What was Ben Howard, premier bachelor, doing pounding on her door?

Melinda's heart was racing. She'd admired Ben in high school. He was a flawless package of sheer masculinity.

"What in the blazes do you call this?"

Her caller was shaking the morning newspaper under her nose.

Local Businessman To Marry Childhood Sweetheart.

Beneath the headline, Melinda caught a glimpse of her name coupled with Ben's. The words were too familiar to ignore. No wonder he was so angry. It was what she deserved for giving in to a wedding fantasy and choosing him for the groom.

She was going to faint. Before she could fall, Ben caught her. Even through her distress, she felt herself respond to his touch.

Melinda sagged in his arms. "I have no idea how that got in there!"

But she did. She did.

Dear Reader,

Come join us for another dream-fulfilling month of Harlequin American Romance! We're proud to have this chance to bring you our four special new stories.

In her brand-new miniseries, beloved author Cathy Gillen Thacker will sweep you away to Laramie, Texas, hometown of matchmaking madness for THE LOCKHARTS OF TEXAS. Trouble brews when arch rivals Beau and Dani discover a marriage license—with their names on it! Don't miss *The Bride Said, "I Did?"*!

What better way to turn a bachelor's mind to matrimony than sending him a woman who desperately needs to have a baby? Mindy Neff continues her legendary BACHELORS OF SHOTGUN RIDGE miniseries this month with *The Horseman's Convenient Wife*—watch Eden and Stony discover that love is anything but convenient!

Imagine waking up to see your own wedding announcement in the paper—to someone you hardly know! Melinda has some explaining to do to Ben in Mollie Molay's *The Groom Came C.O.D.*, the first book in our HAPPILY WEDDED AFTER promotion. And in Kara Lennox's *Virgin Promise*, a bad boy is shocked to discover he's seduced a virgin. Will promising to court her from afar convince her he wants more than one night of passion?

Find out this month, only from Harlequin American Romance!

Best wishes,
Melissa Jeglinski
Associate Senior Editor

The Groom
Came C.O.D.

MOLLIE MOLAY

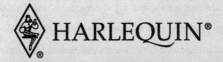

HARLEQUIN®

TORONTO • NEW YORK • LONDON
AMSTERDAM • PARIS • SYDNEY • HAMBURG
STOCKHOLM • ATHENS • TOKYO • MILAN • MADRID
PRAGUE • WARSAW • BUDAPEST • AUCKLAND

For Harrison Ty Bauer.
Now there are eight. Welcome.

ISBN 0-373-16839-X

THE GROOM CAME C.O.D.

Copyright © 2000 by Mollie Molé.

This edition published by arrangement with Harlequin Books S.A.

Visit us at www.eHarlequin.com

Printed in U.S.A.

ABOUT THE AUTHOR

After working for a number of years as a logistics contract administrator in the aircraft industry, Mollie Molay turned to a career she found far more satisfying—writing romance novels. Mollie lives in Northridge, California, surrounded by her two daughters and eight grandchildren, many of whom find their way into her books. She enjoys hearing from her readers and welcomes comments. You can write to her at Harlequin Books, 300 East 42ⁿᵈ St., 6ᵗʰ Floor, New York, NY 10017.

Books by Mollie Molay

HARLEQUIN AMERICAN ROMANCE

Miss Melinda Carey

and

Mr. Ben Howard

are pleased to invite you to their wedding on

Saturday, August 5

at 8 p.m.

at the Oak Tree Distillery, Ojai, California.

Proudly giving their niece and nephew

in marriage are

Miss Bertilda Blanchard

and

Mr. Joseph Howard.

Prologue

Melinda Carey skimmed the dismal financial data on her computer screen. There was no doubt about it—the bridal shop was slowly but surely sliding into a sea of red ink.

It was the second week in June—traditionally, the most popular time for weddings. A time when romantic hearts and minds were supposed to turn to thoughts of weddings, home, hearth and family. But what should have been the shop's busy season looked as if it were going to be the slowest month of the year.

August, the second most popular month, didn't look as if it were going to be an improvement. And no matter how difficult it was to face, the rest of the year looked alarmingly bare.

"It wasn't supposed to be this way," Melinda muttered as she changed screens to check future bookings. Not in the bridal business, anyway. Things had been different before local brides had decided to shop in nearby Santa Barbara.

The screen told the story; after years of comfortable

income, Bertie's Bridal Shop and Bridal Referral Service hung precariously on the brink of bankruptcy.

Melinda gazed out the window at the small park across the street. Newly watered spring greenery sparkled under the bright morning sunshine. Red, purple and white petunias lined gravel paths. Rose bushes displayed all their glory.

She'd always loved the little walk-in park. She'd fantasized about getting married under the weeping willow tree that hung gracefully over the newly painted white gazebo. Fat chance. The way her life was headed, her dream didn't have a chance.

It hadn't been for the lack of a suitor, she thought sadly. She'd been engaged to the man she'd worked for in San Francisco, and they were about to set the wedding date. Luckily, she'd discovered Paul was self-centered and self-serving before it was too late.

Now there was her Aunt Bertie to consider. What man in his right mind would want to take on a thirty-something spinster and her fey aunt—Ojai's beloved town character?

She willed the figures on the monitor to change. Instead, they remained solidly in the red. Not even the bridal referral service she'd started a few months ago managed to turn red ink into black. With no ready answers to the financial problems facing her, her thoughts wandered.

She was thirty, almost thirty-one. Single, with no prospective groom in sight. Let alone a man she was attracted to. Her biological clock was ticking loudly. Loudly enough to keep her awake at night. Almost without deliberate thought, her fingers surfed the Net, creating a dream wedding of her own.

No groom? No problem. Her bridal referral library service had access to every possible item a bride could want. After all, this was a harmless fantasy, wasn't it?

Her fingers raced over the computer keys and clicked onto a dating service Web site. In seconds, she was looking at photographs of men available to ''rent'' for all occasions. Including that of a stand-in groom for wedding rehearsals. She gasped as she took a second look at a new entrant, tall, athletic, blue-eyed Ben Howard.

He was an older version of the boy she'd had a secret crush on in high school. The school's top athlete, Ben had been the handsome hero of every young girl's dream. Including hers.

Drawn to him in a way that still made her blush, she couldn't take her eyes off the screen. To her dismay, his eyes seemed to bore into hers with a message she found herself responding to. The faint smile that hovered at his lips sent heat rushing through her middle.

Her hormones raced as she recalled the single dance they'd shared at a high school Sadie Hawkins Day party years ago, when the girls chose their partners instead of waiting to be asked. At the time, he was the high school's star basketball player. She had been a silent, adoring fan.

Even today, she could feel his strong arms around her as he whirled her around the dance floor. She'd been lost in a dream world—until he'd planted a chaste kiss on her forehead and told her he'd see her around.

Twelve years later, here he was again. And although he was only a photograph on a screen, he was still the man of her choice. She studied his image wistfully.

She'd heard he'd gotten married and divorced while he was still in college. Maybe that was the reason there was something about the determined look in his eyes and the edge in his body language that told her he'd turned into a no-nonsense type, definitely not given to indulging in romantic dreams. For sure, he'd changed from the laughing young boy she remembered to the sober, socially prominent and wealthy distillery owner.

What was he doing on a dating Web site?

Still, there he was. Large as life—and for hire. Since this was only a fantasy, she chose him. No one would ever know.

The date of the ceremony? The sooner the better. With an eye on the calendar, she chose a date one month away.

The location? The small walk-in park, of course.

The wedding dress? No problem there, either. A simple three-quarter-length sheer silk slip-dress with pink and pale-green hand-embroidered flowers and a matching jacket from the bridal shop. A simple wreath of pink roses for her hair.

The minister? The Reverend Charles Good, a longtime friend of Aunt Bertie's.

Deep in her fantasy, she included a caterer to provide a picnic lunch of turkey sandwiches, fresh veggies, fruit and cookies.

Flowers? The local nursery to provide gardenia bushes.

Her excitement grew as she drafted and ''sent'' an announcement to the local newspaper.

The telephone rang. ''Melinda!'' a plaintive female voice moaned. ''You're never going to believe what's happened! You've got to do something to help me!''

With her eyes on the monitor screen, Melinda asked absently, ''What's wrong, Sue Ellen? Your wedding is all taken care of. There can't be anything left to worry about.''

''Frank is allergic to live flowers!''

Melinda's fingers froze above the computer keys. ''He can't be! Not at a time like this! Your wedding is only two days away!''

''He is! He couldn't breathe when I took him to the flower shop this morning to show him the flowers I ordered for the church! I thought he was going to faint! When I finally got him into the fresh air, he told me he's allergic to all kinds of flowers!''

With Sue Ellen Fry's wedding only two days away, Melinda knew she had to move fast. She improvised mentally. ''Don't worry. I'm sure I can locate enough silk flowers here and in Santa Barbara to decorate the church!''

''But my bridal bouquet! And the bridesmaids'

bouquets!'' her caller wailed. ''I can't get married without flowers!''

''I'll think of something for you and the brides-maids. And for Frank to wear in his lapel. Don't worry, Sue Ellen. I'll take care of everything. Just make sure you and Frank are at the church on time.''

She hurriedly set her fantasy wedding aside to turn her attention to the problems confronting a real-life bride.

A quick trip out of town was clearly in order.

Chapter One

The pounding on the front door was loud enough to wake Sleeping Beauty.

Still groggy after a weekend spent scrounging for every silk flower arrangement within a fifty-mile range of Ojai, Melinda stopped in mid-stride on her way to the kitchen. Thank goodness she was invisible to whomever was determined to break down the door. Maybe the caller would give up and go away if she didn't answer.

She was frazzled. She'd been coping with a wedding featuring a disappointed bride, an allergic groom and eight bridesmaids who couldn't seem to understand why they had to carry small white prayer books decorated with sprays of silk lilies of the valley.

Footing the extra cost for silk flowers hadn't helped. She had to figure out a way to return the live flowers so she wouldn't lose the slim profit Bertie's Bridal Shop would eventually realize on the wedding.

The pounding on the door escalated. So did her headache. Her eyes misted with pain. She couldn't take much more.

She glanced at her watch; it was barely eight o'clock—the shop downstairs wasn't scheduled to open for another hour. For that matter, she wasn't properly dressed for company. Considering the monster of a headache she was nursing, whomever was out there would have to wait until she had a cup of hot, ink-black coffee to clear her head.

The pounding became frantic. In the background she could hear a male voice—swearing? *That* tore it! The last thing she needed to cope with right now was an impatient salesman. Anyone who didn't have the sense to realize it was too early to do business with her was out of luck, and she intended to tell him so.

She tied her sleeveless white shirt in a knot at her waist. Made sure her favorite old denim cutoffs covered her bottom and threw open the door.

The next thing she knew, her caller was shaking the morning newspaper under her nose.

"What in the blazes do you call this?"

"I'm afraid there's been some mistake. I haven't reported a missing paper, but thank you anyway." She would have hollered back and given him a dose of his own medicine but someone was pounding on an iron anvil in her head. She started to close the door, but his foot was in the way.

"Of course not! I found your copy on your doorstep!" He thrust the open paper at her.

Ignoring the paper, she looked into eyes that seemed vaguely familiar. "Ben? Ben Howard?"

She gulped as she peered through her pain. The scar at the corner of the caller's lips was white, his eyes breathed fire. What was Ben Howard, the premier bachelor of Ojai, doing pounding on her door at eight o'clock in the morning? She closed her eyes and counted to ten. Maybe he would go away.

It didn't seem to help. Her heart was pounding too fast, and it wasn't from anger. She'd admired Ben years ago in high school and on the dating Web site, but her reaction to his electronic presence paled now that they were face-to-face again. He was a flawless package of sheer masculinity and the last man she expected to see on her doorstep.

"Who else did you think it would be after the wedding announcement I found in the paper?"

Melinda swallowed hard. An uneasy feeling swept over her. This was definitely *not* a social visit. She took a step backward and tried to hide between a wall of affronted dignity. "I don't know what you're talking about. There's obviously been some mistake."

"Oh, there's been a mistake all right, and it looks as if you made it!" He elbowed his way through the door. "I want to know the meaning behind this!"

She suppressed a moan of pain and took another step backward. "I'm sorry, but I still don't know what you're talking about."

"Like hell you don't!" He pointed an accusing finger at the offending article.

Melinda willed herself to remain calm. Maybe if she read the article he would leave. She reached for the paper and squinted at the offending article: Local Businessman To Marry Childhood Sweetheart.

Beneath the headline, she caught a glimpse of her

name coupled with his. The words were too familiar
to ignore. No wonder he was so angry. It was what
she deserved for giving in to a wedding fantasy and
choosing him for the groom.

The pounding in her head became stronger than
ever. She closed her eyes and felt ready to faint from
pain. Before she could fall, Ben caught her. Even
through her distress, she felt herself respond to his
scent of coffee and masculine anger.

Melinda sagged in his arms. She felt like a Rag-
gedy Ann doll, but she matched him glare for glare.
He didn't seem intimidated, so she handed him back
the newspaper. "I have no idea how that got in
there!" But, she did. She did.

"If you don't know who put this in the newspaper,
who does?" He read the article out loud while she
fought for a sensible answer.

"Melinda Carey, I guess that's you," he said with
a cold glance, "a former local resident who recently
returned to take up residence in our little community
with her well-known aunt, Bertilda Blanchard, has announced her engagement and upcoming marriage to
Benjamin Howard.

"Ms. Carey assists her aunt in managing Bertie's
Bridal Shop and its Bridal Referral Service. Mr. How-
ard is a prominent vintner and owner of the Oak Tree
Brandy Distillery." He stopped long enough to scowl.

"The Carey-Howard nuptials are scheduled for
July 4th and will be celebrated outdoors in Sunlight
Park on Main Street."

He lowered the paper and peered at Melinda.

"There's more of this garbage, and what I think of it doesn't bear repeating." He glared. "Why pick on me? I don't even know you!"

To her growing discomfiture, his gaze roved over her bare legs, worked its way up past her thighs to her bare midriff and to her flaming cheeks. He paused. "Or do I?"

Melinda fought a growing dismay and a faint sense of déjà vu. Childhood sweethearts? Ben Howard hadn't spoken to her in years, let alone qualified as a sweetheart. He'd never even held her in his arms—except for the one memorable high school dance they'd shared years ago. He probably didn't remember that, either.

They hadn't been close, not when they were in high school, and definitely not now. She tried to think of an alibi, but all she could think of was the wedding fantasy she'd been toying with on her computer. She couldn't possibly have put it into action, could she?

"Maybe it's just overzealous reporting?" she ventured into his scowl.

He didn't look as if he were buying the explanation, but the way he was eyeing her was another matter.

She tried to ignore him and went back to her mental drawing board.

A wedding at her favorite park across the street?

Her thoughts flew back to her computer musings. She couldn't have! Oh no! She'd done the unthinkable! She stared at Ben uneasily. What would he do if she confessed to fooling around with a wedding fantasy on her computer? That she'd found him on a dating Web site and had chosen him as her groom because she'd never quite gotten over her crush on him.

"So, do I know you?"

"Er…sort of." She smiled weakly. "I'm Melinda Carey. We were in high school together." He shook his head. "I was a junior, you were a senior."

She closed her eyes and steeled herself for another blast of anger. When none came, she slowly opened her eyes. To her chagrin, he was regarding her with a hint of masculine approval.

"You sure have a great imagination, Melinda Carey. I'll give you that much." He studied her meaningfully until goose bumps rose at the back of her neck. "How could I have managed to forget you?"

She found herself staring back at him. His eyes were the blue of memory, only deeper and wiser. He'd matured into a tall, athletic man; he was even more sexy as a grown-up than he'd been as a boy. He'd been the subject of her dreams when she was a teenager. Now that she was older and more experienced, he was still the man she dreamed of.

Her youthful crush on him had been a boy-girl thing, an infatuation with the high school's star athlete. What she felt for him now was pure woman-man attraction.

As if that wasn't enough, one moment he was fit to be tied over some stupid mistake she'd made, and the next moment he was sending her a male seal of approval!

"Probably because you were too busy with that blond cheerleader who took you to that Sadie Hawkins dance," she retorted before she stopped to think. At the look that came into his eyes, she could have bitten her tongue. How could she have said something so inane? So stupid? If he didn't already think something was wrong with her, he was sure to think so now.

His eyebrows rose, a smile curved at his lips. "Ah, Melinda Carey, I may have forgotten you," he said suggestively, "but it looks as if you haven't forgotten me."

She felt herself flush.

"Is that why you put the wedding announcement in the paper? To get even with me ten years later? And why pick now?"

She took a deep breath and started over. "No, of course not. I don't even know why I remembered the dance, or why I even mentioned it. I haven't thought about the dance in years."

He looked incredulous. "So why *did* you do it?"

"The truth is, I was fooling around planning a make-believe wedding on the Internet when I saw your photograph on a dating Web site. I figured if you were available for a date, you'd be available for an imaginary groom."

If he'd looked angry before, he looked furious now. "A dating Web site?" He reared back and frowned. "No way! You're putting me on!"

"It's true, honest. I chose you for an imaginary wedding, not a real one. Why would I lie about it?"

"Beats me. You haven't made any sense up until now, either. How could I get on a dating Web site without my knowledge?"

"I don't know, but it was there," she protested weakly. "All I did was choose you for my groom for my wedding fantasy when I saw your picture."

"Why me?" he repeated. "You could have chosen anyone!"

Melinda thought rapidly. How could she tell him he'd been her idea of a perfect mate ever since she'd first laid eyes on him in high school? That she had even dreamed of him as a perfect husband and father? Or that when she'd seen his image, she jumped at the chance to make him her fantasy groom.

He looked angrier than ever. She hurried to put out the fire growing in his eyes. "I'm sorry about the announcement. I just realized I must have pressed the enter button on my computer by mistake after I was interrupted by a client. It doesn't mean anything. After all, it was only a fantasy wedding."

"A fantasy wedding? You've got to be kidding! Whose?"

"Mine," she answered defiantly. "But I swear I didn't intend to put it into action!"

"You didn't mean to do it?" He waved the newspaper at her. "Hell! That's a weak excuse considering the possible damage you've done."

She continued to protest her innocence, all the time knowing she was as guilty as hell. "Well, it's true. I told you it was unintentional! I pressed the enter button by mistake."

His eyebrows rose until they met. She smiled weakly.

He examined her thoughtfully. Under his studied gaze, her hormones stood at attention. She self-consciously checked the buttons on her blouse.

"About this dating Web site thing," he finally said. "How could you believe I would have agreed to anything so stupid?"

"Maybe not, but your picture's there!"

"So, take it off!"

"Quit hollering," she said, with a glance over her shoulder. "I keep telling you I didn't put you on there! Why can't you believe me?"

"Because you haven't made any sense since I got here." He lowered his voice, but his frustration showed. "In fact the whole story sounds as if you made it all up."

"Kind of, but I'm in no condition to discuss this any further." She gestured to the door. "I have a splitting headache, so if you don't mind, I'd like to be alone."

"Alone to do what? Create more havoc on your computer?"

"No, I intend to have several cups of strong, ink-black coffee. Then I'm going to get dressed and try to go to work. If you insist, I'll get back to you later."

"You mean that's not your working outfit?" His gaze roamed over her with blatant honesty. It was obvious he liked what he saw and was man enough to show it. She shook her head and fought off an urge to cover herself. It was her territory, wasn't it?

"Too bad." He glanced at the mahogany staircase. "You live here?"

Melinda nodded carefully. "With my Aunt Bertie. She owns the shop." The dull ache in her head had turned into a crescendo of pain. She wasn't going to give him the satisfaction of seeing her holding her head to keep it from falling off. Things were bad enough.

His gaze swung back to her. He glanced at the newspaper and raked his fingers through his hair. "I hope you realize you may have blown it big time. How are you going to get us out of this mess."

"There is no 'us,'" she protested. "It was all a mistake. I'm sure everyone will understand when I tell them so. Now, please leave. I honestly can't discuss this right now."

He stepped closer, his now hard blue eyes bore into hers. "Well, *I* can. Why don't you start at the beginning of this mess and give me the whole nine yards."

"It's a long story," she said. "But honestly, I'm in no condition to discuss it. Not right now. I'll get back to you."

"*You're* in no condition?" he barked. "You call it a mistake, but how do you think I feel? I've acquired a fiancée and a wedding date with a bride I don't even know!"

"Please," Melinda protested. She massaged her temples. "I have a terrible headache. You'll have to wait. I'll do something about it. I just don't know what."

Her heart skipped a beat when his gaze softened.

"Okay. I'm willing to compromise. Go ahead and have your coffee. But after you're through I expect you to call the newspaper and retract the announcement. But I warn you, we're not through talking."

Melinda closed her eyes and swallowed hard. How could she carry on an intelligent conversation, let alone try to convince him she had all her marbles when she wasn't all that sure herself? What she needed was to have time to figure out a way to undo the mess she was in.

So much for raging hormones.

Her head pounded. She tried to put one and one together. Before she'd left to rescue a client and her allergic fiancé, she must have pressed the enter button on her computer! Her fantasy wedding plans must have gone into action, including the newspaper announcement. She peered at Ben through a mist of pain. High school sweethearts, of all things! No wonder Ben looked ready to throttle her.

She was heartsick. How could she have gotten so careless as to chose Ojai's most eligible bachelor for a fantasy husband—even by mistake?

Things got even worse when she envisioned the orders she must have placed and supplier's cancellation penalties to follow. And, horror of horrors, the public apology it looked as if she would have to make before Ben was satisfied.

"As long as you insist, come on in the kitchen," she said over her shoulder. "I'll put on the coffee, but I don't guarantee it won't taste like mud."

"Good! I could use something strong right now.

You have no idea of the mess you've created or the attention I'm bound to get because of it.''

Sure, Melinda thought to herself. The number of disappointed women who had set their hopes on winning Ben for a husband were bound to be legion. Considering that he hadn't been in a hurry to take any of them up on it, maybe he should have been grateful to her for getting him off the marriage market.

She was ready to tell him so when the sound of footsteps coming down the wooden stairs interrupted her. Her aunt Bertie tripped into the kitchen.

''Ah, there you are, Benjamin!'' She cocked her head to one side and smiled at Ben and Melinda. ''How sweet of you to come over early to see your fiancée.''

Fiancée? Ben hesitated. The word made his hackles rise, but considering who he was talking to, he bit back the words he was tempted to say. ''Not really, Ms. Bertie. I came as soon as I discovered your niece and I had a lot to discuss.''

He felt himself blush like a teenager when she smiled and glanced at the newspaper crushed in his hand. ''I must tell you how good I felt to see your pending wedding announcement in there! Frankly,'' she said with an admiring glance at Ben, ''I didn't even know you and Melinda were seeing each other, let alone planning to wed. How romantic.''

Ben nodded politely, but his mind cringed at the timing of Bertie's entrance. This was no time to finish reading Melinda the riot act. Nor was it a good time to insist she call the newspaper with a retraction. He'd have to wait until the excitement died down before he had a calm and serious heart-to-heart talk with her. Before he was through, she'd never pull a fool stunt like this again.

As for Bertie, she was a staunch supporter of the high school's athletic teams and the basketball team just as he was. She'd baked her famous chocolate-chip cookies for the high school's fund-raisers as far back as when he'd been a kid. He owed her respect.

Her niece—well, that was another story. He should have been angry with Melinda, but somehow he wasn't any longer.

He glanced over at Melinda. In spite of her headache, with her blond hair caught back in a ponytail and dressed in a brief outfit that revealed as much as it concealed, she looked as fresh and pretty as a spring sunrise.

"I'm so happy for you both," Bertie cried when he bit his lip. "Especially for you, Melinda. I know you tried to keep the wedding a secret, but the truth is that I've known about it since Friday." She beamed proudly.

"How could you have known? I didn't tell anyone!" Melinda's heart took a dive at the innocent smile that came over her aunt's face. The premonition she wasn't going to like her aunt's answer was as strong as the anvil beating in her head. "How did you find out?"

"Martha Ebbetts called me when she got the e-mail message." She beamed at Ben. "I'm sure you know that Martha is the society editor of the *Ojai*

Newsday. Anyway, Martha called here Saturday. When she heard Melinda wasn't home she asked me for some filler for her article.''

''Filler?'' Melinda gasped.

''Article, Ms. Bertie?''

''Yes, of course. Martha wanted to add some human interest to the announcement. I was thrilled to be able to oblige.''

''Aunt Bertie—you didn't! Tell me you didn't tell Martha anything!''

Ben glanced over at Melinda. The water in the coffeepot she held in her hand sloshed over the brim. Her face had turned white. Hell, she looked ready to faint again. He sprang into action, grabbed the glass coffeepot, put it on the sink and threw his arm around her shoulders. ''Just what was it you told Martha Ebbetts, Ms. Bertie?''

Melinda's aunt put a forefinger to her lips and appeared to think for a minute or two. By the time she was ready with an answer, he was a nervous wreck.

''Why, I just told Martha you've known knew each other since high school. I *was* right about that, wasn't I?''

Ben swore under his breath. Bertie looked so innocent, it was hard for him to believe she could be serious. Considering she'd known him as a high school student, she must have known he and Melinda were practically strangers. ''Maybe, but that's a long way from being sweethearts, wouldn't you say?''

Bertie smiled happily. ''Martha wanted to spice up the story a wee bit. Calling you childhood sweethearts does tend to make the story more romantic, don't you think?''

He heard Melinda groan softly. From long experience as a local businessman, he knew exactly what she was thinking. If anyone could pump up a story and turn it into a fairy tale, it was the legendary Martha Ebbetts, a contemporary of Bertie's. But one thing was clear; whatever else Melinda had done, at least she hadn't labeled them high school sweethearts.

''You have no idea just how the announcement is going to sound to some people, Ms. Bertie. Or what a few of them might think when they get around to reading it,'' he added slowly. ''But I suppose there's not much I can do about it now.'' He glanced at the stack of bridal magazines on the kitchen table and became aware of the soft music that was filtering through the intercom. Coupled with the bridal paraphernalia that filled the front rooms, the house was a potential hotbed for hopeless romantics. What else should he have expected from Melinda and her aunt?

Bottom line, he didn't intend to be caught up in a fantasy wedding, harmless or not. Let alone one Melinda had apparently broadcast to the world on the Internet! When things calmed down, he intended to take care of whomever had put him on that damn Web site she talked about.

Melinda broke the silence. By nature, the last thing she wanted to do was to hurt anyone. Including Ben, who was after all an innocent party to her mistake. ''It was all a mistake, Aunt Bertie. Ben and I aren't engaged to be married, honest.''

Her aunt tittered. "A wedding is a poor thing to joke about, dear."

"I'm not joking, Aunt Bertie." Melinda glanced at Ben for support. This time he was listening, thank goodness.

"I'm afraid I was playing around with my wedding fantasy on the computer," Melinda explained. "I planned the whole wedding, including the announcement to the newspaper." She ran a trembling hand over her forehead. "I wasn't aware I'd set my daydream into action until Ben showed up. But now that we know what happened, why don't we all just forget it and go on? I'll try to think of a way to correct my mistake."

"I wish, but I'm afraid it's not that easy. Not after the newspaper announcement," Ben muttered as he envisioned the telephone calls waiting for him when he got home. Calls from his country club friends— hell, he could handle those by treating it all as a joke. The expected telephone call from his uncle Joseph, was something else. His uncle, his only remaining relative, had been after him to remarry. He'd have to think fast to keep from disappointing him one more time.

Ben paced the floor, his thoughts in turmoil. He couldn't think of a damn suggestion to help Melinda straighten out the mess she'd made of things. But first things first. "You'll have to call Martha Ebbetts and retract the story. The sooner the better. I'll try to think of some kind of alibi as to why we're calling off the wedding."

"Absolutely not," Bertie broke in briskly. "Any cancellation of the wedding would bring you both bad luck. No matter how it started, I believe this wedding was destined to happen or Melinda wouldn't have pushed that whateveryoucallit button on the computer. As for what prompted her to do it, maybe a higher and wiser power than we was behind it."

"Aunt Bertie! You can't possibly be serious!"

"I certainly am," her aunt replied firmly. "One ought not to argue with destiny, you know," she warned, shaking her finger at Melinda. "Besides, I've always been fond of you, Benjamin. I think a marriage between you and Melinda is a splendid idea."

"Thank you, and I appreciate the way you feel. But this wedding business is something different." Ben cringed inside. He had mental visions of Aunt Bertie baking a mountain of chocolate-chip cookies for the wedding. As for her regaling wedding guests with stories of his days as the star of the high school's basketball team, there were a few escapades he would rather forget. It was time to set the record straight even if he was tempting fate.

"The truth is, I don't want to be any part of this." He shot Melinda a hard look that belied his earlier softening. "I have my reasons for asking you to call off this so-called wedding. The sooner the better."

"I wish I knew how," Melinda said over her aunt's protests. "No matter what I do, it's going to raise a lot of questions." She bit her bottom lip. "Maybe we ought to go through a pretend ceremony?"

"No way! As a matter of fact, I've never been so

sure of anything in my life,'' he answered grimly. ''The wedding is off!''

At the final note in Ben's voice, Melinda felt more miserable than ever. It wasn't only her headache that wouldn't allow her to think clearly, it was Ben. The star basketball player in high school had been happy-go-lucky, full of innocent fun and laughter. And very aware of his sexy impact on all the girls. To her dismay, he had the same impact now. ''You're sure you want me to call everything off?''

''Damn sure.''

Visions of more problems for the struggling bridal shop once her retraction was out tumbled through Melinda's mind. She'd be the laughing stock of Ojai.

She started to explain again then stopped. It was useless. There was no room for argument in Ben's unbending body language. She'd have to face the music and hope for the best.

''If you won't change your mind,'' she answered with as much dignity she could muster, ''I'll try to take care of everything as soon as I get dressed.''

''Good.'' Ignoring the unhappy look in Melinda's eyes and her aunt's reproachful gaze, Ben made his way past the two front rooms that had been turned into a bridal shop. The sight of cases full of wedding paraphernalia made him clench his teeth.

On his left, in what would have been a parlor in earlier days, were open boxes of white satin shoes and glass cases filled with matching beaded bags and other accessories. A glass case displayed bridal headpieces, strings of pearls and small gifts for the bride to give to her attendants.

The room to the right of him was lined with flowing white and pastel gowns for brides, bridesmaids and for mothers-of-the bride. A mannequin dressed as a bride with a flowing veil and a bridal bouquet in her arms seemed to gaze at him with a look of reproach as he passed.

His conscience stirred; for a moment he almost hesitated and turned back to the kitchen to explain himself. To explain why he was so against marriage. Until he recalled that the bottom line was that he couldn't afford to care or, real or not, he would find himself a married man.

As for Bertie and her niece, they might live in a dream world of happily-ever-after, but there was no happily-ever-after in the real world he'd lived in. His misbegotten marriage when he'd been a senior in college had proved that to him. He knew from bitter experience there were no happy endings when it came to marriage—real or otherwise. Not before and certainly not now.

Chapter Two

Ben got as far as the entrance to the small park across the street from the bridal shop before he came to a stop.

He felt like a heel leaving Melinda and her aunt without a decent explanation for his attitude. Not that it would be easy to explain when he wasn't even sure he understood why himself. His earlier marriage had taken place years ago, but that was then and this was now.

Maybe he should have been grateful for the unexpected turn of events. Maybe now he could get rid of all the wannabe Mrs. Ben Howards.

Shaken out of his reverie by a flock of birds bursting from the full branches of the tree above him, he found himself gazing around him. It was the setting where, according to the wedding announcement, he was scheduled to marry Melinda next month.

The scent of jasmine filled the air. Rustic bridges crossed a babbling brook that slowly meandered through the small park. Carefully tended green hedges bordered the cobblestone walks that led to a white lattice gazebo in the park's center. A sundial, a bird-bath and white iron benches were scattered throughout the small park. It was the last place in the world he expected to find himself. Let alone find himself taking Melinda seriously.

What had brought him here when he had more important things that needed his attention? And why was he suddenly so unsure of his decision to have the fantasy wedding called off?

He thought of Bertie's assurance that a higher power was at work. Was there some kind of magic aura in the early morning air that made her pronouncement sound reasonable? Was it the same aura that was urging him to go back and tell Melinda he was thinking of changing his mind? That he didn't want to call off the wedding? And why did it suddenly seem as if it were the right thing to do?

His thoughts stopped him cold. After all, he was an intelligent and successful businessman. Why was he even thinking of magic auras? Was he losing it?

Something turned him back to gaze at the vintage Victorian house across the street. Bertie's Bridal Shop had been housed there for more years than he could remember. He remembered his two older sisters had purchased their bridal gowns there years ago.

The brown wooden house with its faded white trim was showing its age. The porch railings sagged, but freshly starched lace curtains proudly graced the windows. It looked familiar, and yet there was something different about it today that caught his attention. He squinted in the sunshine to get a better look. The let-

tering on the sign in the window that advertised a
Bridal Referral Service was fairly new. According to
Bertie, the service was Melinda's attempt to keep the
shop in the black. The idea may have sounded like a
good idea, but there were screwups every day on the
Internet.

The realization that she'd found him on an Internet
dating service turned his blood to ice water. He
should have looked into how it got there before he
left. If word got out that Melinda had found him there,
he was a dead man.

Before he could decide what prompted him to re-
trace his footsteps, he found himself back at the bridal
shop's front door. He was about to knock when he
remembered Melinda's headache. He rang the doorbell—gently, but firmly. He had a mission to accom-
plish.

The door opened a few inches. Bertie peered out.
"I knew you'd be back as soon as you had a chance
to think things over, Benjamin." She held the door
open with a welcoming smile. "I baked your favorite
cookies last night. Why don't you come in and join
me in a fresh cup of coffee?"

Ben glanced over her shoulder at the empty entry.
"Actually, Ms. Bertie, I came back to talk to Melinda."

"Of course," she agreed amicably. Come right in.
Your bride is upstairs getting dressed. She'll be down
in a minute."

His bride! It was the last thing he wanted to hear,
at least until he had a chance to talk things over with

Melinda. "Sorry, Ms. Bertie. This bride stuff is a little premature."

She wagged her forefinger at him. "Now, Benjamin, you aren't still having cold feet, are you?"

He shook his head. Why wasn't he heading for the safety of his distillery where more rational heads prevailed instead of talking to a wall? "Not really. The fact is, I came back to apologize for losing my temper. It's just that I was sure the wedding announcement would play havoc with my life. Even now," he added with a wry shrug as he followed her into the kitchen, "I feel as if I'm caught in the middle of a hornet's nest."

She smiled and prattled on about reluctant bridegrooms.

Maybe it was the odor of freshly brewed coffee or the plate of chocolate-chip cookies waiting on the kitchen table, but Ben felt right at home. The bright-yellow and white chintz curtains at the windows were invitations to enjoy a few moments of relaxation. Under different circumstances, he would have been ready. Unfortunately, the soft music coming over the intercom designed to calm bridal nerves wasn't exactly music to his ears.

The muscles at the back of his neck tensed as he dropped into a chair. Bertie's contented smile did nothing to reassure him he was going to make a dent in her conviction that he was about to become a member of her family.

He watched her flutter about the kitchen setting out cups and saucers.

"How did you know I'd be back, Ms. Bertie?" he asked, interrupting a tale that had something to do about a bride having to wrestle a groom to the altar.

Her answering smile was benevolent. "You can't run away from your destiny, dear."

He didn't have a ready reply to that remark.

What was there about the lady that made the illogical seem logical? What was there about her that had him ready to believe in her conviction that destiny had brought him here and not the wedding announcement in the newspaper. Or were they the same?

He was a pragmatic man who had spent his life creating his own destiny. He'd decided the only way to do something for the economy of Ojai was to do it himself. With Bertie happily prattling in the background, his thoughts swung to his Oak Tree Gourmet Distillery, an enterprise he'd started to bring industry to a town that survived largely on tourism. That decision hadn't been decided by fate, as Bertie preached. No, sir. It had been a sure, pragmatic decision and, thank God, it had worked. Oak Tree brandies were known all over the world.

Still, considering he was a visitor in her kitchen, he couldn't tell Bertie he was ready to believe she must have come from a different planet. Or that maybe she could be a guardian angel in disguise. For sure, she was an innocent who saw only the positive side of everything and everyone, including him.

"Ms. Bertie," he began, "I don't know if it was fate or destiny that turned me back here, but the fact is I owe you an apology."

"Of course, dear," she soothed. She moved the plate of plump cookies closer to him. "But, there's no rush. Take your time."

Ben swallowed a sigh. Once the newspaper announcement of his "wedding" hit the streets, there *was* a rush. He was running out of time.

"It's just that you've always been so decent to me—and the whole town, for that matter. I shouldn't have lost my cool. I wouldn't want you to think I've gone off the deep end."

"There's nothing to explain, dear." She patted his shoulder in passing on her way to turn off the coffee. "I understand perfectly. You're just having a bit of bridegroom nerves."

Ben bit back a hollow laugh and tried again. "I don't think you *do* understand, Ms. Bertie. I want you to know I don't hold what Melinda did against her. I came back to tell her so. Everyone makes mistakes, myself included. It's just that I don't understand why Melinda would pick me for her fantasy bridegroom. We hardly know each other."

Bertie smiled over her shoulder. "The answer is there for you to see, Benjamin. All you need to do is open your mind."

"Open my mind?" Ben reared back in his chair. "That's the problem! I have opened it, and I've been in a state of shock ever since I read this morning's newspaper! Marry Melinda? I swear it was the first time I'd heard of it."

Her eyes took on a sparkle. "Perhaps so, but I believe you and Melinda were fated to meet again. It doesn't matter how. Although I have to admit the circumstances are a bit unusual.''

"You got that right," Ben murmured under his breath.

"However, I'm very pleased at Melinda's choice," she went on. "I've always said you're a fine young man."

He would have laughed at her naïveté if she hadn't been so sincere. Bertie wouldn't have seen anything wrong with him even if the truth stared her in the face. "After all the crazy things I managed to get into in high school?"

"Boys are boys," she agreed. "It comes with the territory. But I'm sure what you did then was harmless and not at anyone's expense. Just look at you now! Ojai owes you a great deal for all you've done for us.''

After Bertie's endorsement, he was beginning to think there was a halo blinking above his head. So why didn't he feel saintly?

In the interest of getting out of here before the morning was through, Ben agreed his intentions were good. It wasn't all that much, but every little bit helped. "Thank you. But to get back to why I'm here. I want to set the record straight. I got angry because I hate to be used. Or made to do something I hadn't planned for…like get married."

"If it will make you feel better, go right ahead and get it off your chest." She smiled and waited expectantly. "But I'm all for you and my niece getting married."

Ben took a deep breath. "I want to go on record that I haven't spoken to Melinda in years before now—certainly not since high school. The truth is, I don't remember her. So you see," he went on earnestly, "I couldn't have proposed."

Bertie set a steaming cup of coffee on the table in front of him. "Perhaps. What do you think prompted my niece to plan a marriage to you if fate hadn't prompted her to make her little mistake?"

Little mistake! It was a mistake large enough to change his life!

He munched on a chocolate-filled cookie and gazed around the kitchen. "Maybe, but considering we're knee-deep in bridal territory, I guess it could have been natural for Melinda to play out her dream wedding on the Internet. Maybe it was a harmless fantasy—but it sure backfired. I'm not even sure it'll help even if she does retract the story," he said morosely.

Bertie smiled. "You're thinking of changing your mind about asking Melinda to go ahead with the retraction, aren't you?"

"How did you know?" The way the woman was able to read him was beginning to make him nervous. Why hadn't he left well enough alone and kept on going when he'd left the first time? Why had he given in to the urge to come back to explain himself to someone who was convinced fate was about to make him her nephew?

"By the way, Ms. Bertie, a moment ago you said you expected me to come back. How did you know I would change my mind?"

She answered his question with a question of her own. "You *have* come back, haven't you?"

Ben took a deep swallow of coffee and studied his companion. Did the little park have some magical power that had worked on him? Had it been Bertie herself who had willed him back? He shook his head to clear it. No matter what she might believe about fate and destiny, he for one was living in a real world. He tried again.

"I have to tell you that when I found myself in the park across the street, the strangest feeling came over me, Ms. Bertie. Before I knew it, I found myself back at your door." He shook his head in wonder. "I had the strongest feeling someone was sending me a message."

She beamed at him as if he'd passed some kind of test. "I'm so pleased you feel this way. You see, when Melinda asked you to go along with the wedding, it was more than a matter of pride." She slid the plate of cookies closer to him. "Here, have another cookie."

"Thanks." Years of Bertie's famous cookies had turned him into a cookie addict. "Too bad you aren't running a bakery instead of a bridal shop, Ms. Bertie." *He wouldn't have been in such a mess.* Bertie might be oblivious to the implications of Melinda's wedding announcement, but it was his life they were talking about. "Go ahead."

"The bridal shop is on the verge of bankruptcy," Bertie began slowly, but he could see a hint of sadness in her eyes. Obviously, even guardian angels had human feelings. The knowledge that he might be adding to her unhappiness made him feel worse than ever.

"Melinda doesn't think I know the financial status of the shop, but I do," Bertie went on. "I couldn't let on that I knew the truth. Not when she left a good position in San Francisco to come back to help me. Why," she added proudly, "she's even added a bridal referral service to make ends meet. It has been useful, but I'm afraid there aren't enough interested brides in Ojai. Young women today aren't interested in tradition. They go to a bigger city to shop."

Ben stirred uncomfortably. "I'm truly sorry to hear that, Ms. Bertie. I remember my sisters telling me how helpful you were with their weddings."

"Thank you, Benjamin, it's kind of you to say so. The fact is that because of the state of my finances, Melinda is afraid any unusual or adverse publicity would hurt the little business I do have left. So you see, by asking you to go along with her, she was only trying to protect me."

Now Ben really felt like a worm. If only Melinda's make-believe wedding hadn't involved him, he might even have thought the caper was amusing. Now, after hearing Bertie's story, the picture was changing. The problem was more than Melinda's pride—Bertie's future was at stake. Damn!

As if sensing his mixed emotions, Bertie leaned over and patted his hand. "It's not your fault Melinda's fantasy went awry, dear boy. I believe that there's another reason that prompted her to set her fantasy in motion.'' Her blue eyes lightened as she gazed fondly at him. ''I believe this is a moment to give you both a second chance to fulfill your destinies. Fate brought you two together.''

Ben felt shivers run up and down his spine. He was in between a rock and a hard place. He didn't want to remarry, not yet. And certainly not after his earlier marriage had been such a sorry experience. There was also his uncle Joseph who was after him to marry and start a family. And women at the country club who seemed to be set on being his wife.

Maybe a make-believe marriage to Melinda Carey *could* be the answer.

Then, too, from what he understood, there was Bertie. She could lose everything she'd spent a lifetime working for.

He struggled for an answer, but one thing was clear. It was beginning to look as if he might be damned if he went through with the wedding and damned if he didn't.

''Aunt Bertie! Ben! What's going on?''

Ben jumped to his feet as Melinda rushed into the room. Bertie calmly motioned him back to his seat. ''I was just explaining the situation to Benjamin, dear.''

Melinda was horrified. To her, ''situation'' could mean only one thing. ''Aunt Bertie, please tell me you didn't!''

Her aunt's guilty look was all the answer Melinda needed. She turned her gaze on the noncommittal look on Ben's face. Her aunt not only knew the truth about her financial affairs, it looked as if she'd shared the information with him!

"What are you doing back here, Ben Howard? I've already agreed I would call Martha Ebbetts and retract my announcement, haven't I? What more do you want?"

"Yes, well..." He seemed to struggle for an answer, but whatever he wanted to say wasn't coming easily. "I was just about to say that maybe I was too hasty before. In fact, I've been thinking of changing my mind."

Melinda stiffened her back. If this was a marriage proposal, she'd never heard a more reluctant one. "I can just imagine what my aunt told you. Well, let me set you straight. I don't need your pity. My aunt and I have managed to get along until now, and we'll get through this, too."

"Maybe, maybe not," Ben rejoined. He eyed her in a way that made her hormones snap to attention. "But before I commit myself, I have a few thoughts of my own about this marriage you've dreamed up. Maybe we can settle it to our mutual satisfaction."

Mutual satisfaction? The only way she would be satisfied was if Ben Howard took himself out of her sight before she died of embarrassment. "I've just told you it's not necessary."

"Maybe so, but I think you at least owe me the chance to discuss it."

Bertie rose. "Why don't you and Benjamin talk things over quietly, dear. I have an errand or two to take care of.'' She waved goodbye and glided out of the kitchen.

Ben eyed Melinda warily. He was determined to find a way to at least discuss his crazy ideas with her—for both their sakes. Too bad she didn't look as if she were the compromising type.

He plunged in before she could start up again. ''I wanted to explain why the wedding announcement riled me. Okay?'' She nodded reluctantly. ''The truth is I was married once—in college.''

Melinda held up her hand to stop him. ''I've heard all about it. What does it have to do with me?''

''Only that the marriage lasted long enough for Annie and me to realize we were too young to know what we really wanted. When I told her I wanted to go on to grad school and study law, she announced she wasn't willing to wait that long to have a life. The divorce came though the day we graduated.'' He shrugged. ''You might say it was a graduation present.''

''I still don't see what this has to do with me.''

''I was just trying to explain why I reacted the way I did after I read the newspaper this morning.'' He grinned sheepishly. ''I guess you could say I'm allergic to marriage.''

''Great!'' Melinda grimaced. Another allergic bridegroom! ''All the more reason to forget this whole thing.''

Ben bit his lower lip. Hell, *she* was the one who started the mess, why was she so upset? Forget it? Fat chance. ''I'm trying to tell you there's a good reason why a temporary marriage between us might be a good idea.''

"A good idea?" If Ben had said Mars was hurtling its way toward Earth and would arrive in Ojai tomorrow, she wouldn't have been more surprised. "Are you trying to tell me you *want* to get married now?"

"Yes, no...that is, maybe." Ben gazed thoughtfully at his prospective bride. If he'd been looking for another wife, Melinda would certainly fit the bill. She was honest and loyal. She wasn't greedy, either, or she would have jumped at the chance to be the wife of one of Ojai's first families.

Luckily, there was more to admire in Melinda than her character. Her silky legs turned him on. Her womanly curves were pleasing. And so were her expressive green eyes and tossed blond hair.

She wore beige linen slacks and a matching silk blouse, pearls around her throat and at her ears. Definitely a class act. But the shorts and the sleeveless white shirt that left her midriff bare and the lush line of breasts exposed earlier had been a lot more interesting. If she'd been as attractive in high school as she was now, how could he have managed not to notice her?

If he put the facts together and threw caution to the wind, marrying Melinda could make sense. All he had to do was control his testosterone and remember he was planning on a marriage of convenience followed by a quiet annulment.

"If you don't mind," he began again, "I'd like to

tell you something. It's not easy for me to say, but I shouldn't have lost my temper.''

Seemingly speechless, Melinda continued to stare at him. He didn't blame her. He didn't recognize himself in all of this, either. ''If it's okay with you, I'd like to apologize for the things I said earlier.''

Melinda nodded. Reluctantly, but he was relieved to see he had her grudging attention.

''So…maybe we ought to think about this marriage business.''

Melinda looked at him warily. ''Wait a minute! Let me understand this. You're suggesting we actually go through with a wedding ceremony?''

He shrugged. ''Maybe.''

''I can't believe this!'' She let loose. ''Either you do or you don't. First you blow your stack and then you come back here to tell me that you've changed your mind. Let's get this straight—do you want to get married or don't you?''

''Sort of,'' he murmured, caught between a rock and a hard place. ''*Something* changed my mind and brought me back here. I'm just not sure what it was.''

How could he tell her what had turned him back when he hadn't had a logical answer to account for it?

He tried to concentrate on the happy smile on Bertie's face. And the way she'd waved at him before she disappeared through the kitchen door. A blessing?

All the more reason he had to go on record about the conditions of the forthcoming wedding—provided they ultimately decided to go through with it.

"There *is* one thing I'd like to put on the table." Melinda stared at him silently. Good. After what he had to say, he wasn't sure she wasn't going to take things so quietly. "This so-called marriage thing—you didn't intend it to be real. It was only a fantasy. Right?"

Melinda's face turned pink. She nodded hesitantly.

"I hate to get personal," he insisted, "but under the circumstances, I have to be sure you *do* understand what I'm talking about."

Melinda's face turned a deeper pink. "If you're saying this is going to be a marriage of convenience, I never intended anything else. In fact," she frowned, "the more I think of it, the more I know this would never work. We'd have to be crazy."

Ben had the feeling he should have his head examined. Two hours ago he'd gone on record as being against a wedding of any kind and here he was trying to convince Melinda they should go for it. Strangely enough, even though she was giving him a chance to back out, he actually felt disappointed. "The truth is," he blurted, "I might need a wife."

"*Might* need a wife?"

If ever there was a time to admit the whole truth, this was it. "Yes. This might sound crazy, but my uncle has been after me to get married. For that matter," he muttered darkly, "so have a lot of women."

"Lucky you." The look she gave him would have frozen an Eskimo. "Why pick me?"

How could he tell her mistake was opportune? That he sensed she could be trusted to "dissolve" the marriage when the right time came. That it might be convenient to have her as his "wife" for the duration. He managed a grin. "Maybe your timing was right. Or maybe your aunt was right about your 'mistake.' Maybe it *was* fate."

Melinda considered Ben's answer. Her aunt had talked about fate and destiny for so long, she was conditioned to believe it herself. At any rate, a mock-marriage, without a license, to a socially prominent man with connections might just be the ultimate answer to the lack of prospective brides. She didn't have to feel she was using him. From what he'd said, the marriage would be to his advantage, too. "I'll think about it."

"Good, I'm glad we finally agree on something." Ben settled back in his chair. "I think we should also settle a few important details while we're at it. Okay?"

Melinda shrugged. "After the story you just told me, I can't imagine what else is left to talk about. But go ahead."

"I'll supply the minister."

She hesitated. "Actually, if I decide to go through with the wedding I was going to ask the Reverend Charles Good to conduct the ceremony. Charles is a good friend of Aunt Bertie's."

"A real minister?"

"Of course."

"No way!" Ben rose and paced the kitchen floor. He counted off the squares in the brown and white linoleum until his frustration cooled. "I'm not going to take a chance on anything going wrong. I have a friend back in Boston who is a drama professor. Dex will fly out to do the honors if I ask him to. He'll not only look and act like a real minister, there's a plus.''

''What's that,'' she asked cautiously.

''No one will ever see him again.''

''We can't,'' she protested. ''It would break my aunt's heart, and I'd feel like a fraud!''

His eyebrows rose. ''Would you feel any differently if this friend of your aunt's performed a mock-ceremony without a license?''

Melinda glanced down at her clenched hands. Her heart was breaking into little pieces. The dream she'd woven into her fantasy wedding was crumbling fast, and she didn't know how to stop it. A platonic, temporary marriage with a man she'd yearned over for half of her life was the last thing she'd expected. How could she have gotten in so deep?

Ben cleared his throat. He'd never seen a more unhappy look on the face of a woman who had just gotten engaged. He'd have to make it up to her later. ''Sorry. Tell the reverend I'm having a close college friend do the honors. Just be sure he doesn't know the truth. What he and Ms. Bertie don't know won't hurt them.'' He hesitated. ''Oh, one more thing. I want you to take my photograph off that damn dating Web site before anyone else sees it!''

''I told you I had nothing to do with putting it on there!''

''I don't care. If it's not too late, see if you can get me off there before the whole town sees it.''

Chapter Three

Ben headed for his office wondering just what he'd talked himself into.

Built on to a side of the Oak Tree distillery, the office was a refuge where he could let the world, the telephone and the fax machine go by when he was so inclined. After his mind-boggling discussion with Melinda and her aunt, he was definitely inclined.

Shaded by the oak trees that surrounded the building, the office was cool and scented with the rich pungent aroma of fine fruit brandies that were Oak Tree's specialty. On the other side of the office wall, the season's fruit crop was being aged in oak casks until it was ready to be bottled. He took great pride in knowing that the brandies carrying the Oak Tree name were the among the finest dessert liquors on the West Coast. Maybe, in the world.

Educated as a lawyer, he'd quickly discovered practicing law wasn't for him. For an innovative thinker like him, the law had turned out to be more about precedent than creativity. He'd realized he needed to create something tangible. That had translated into utilizing the bountiful fruit orchards on Howard family land. Happily, with his uncle's agreement, the Oak Tree Distillery had been the answer.

He dropped into his well-worn leather chair, stared at the telephone and willed it not to ring. He needed time to pull his thoughts together, to make sense of the day's events—if there was anything sensible about it.

What really worried him was what his uncle would think when he saw the wedding announcement in the morning newspaper. A no-nonsense, dignified man with high standards, as well as an upholder of tradition, Uncle Joseph was bound to have questions. Who wouldn't? He had some himself.

He knew it was too late to worry when his uncle strolled into his office unannounced, the morning's newspaper in his hand. At sixty-five, he still carried himself with dignity. So much so, no one thought to shorten his name to Joe. Not even him. In white linen slacks, light blue shirt and dark blue jacket, he looked every inch the wealthy owner of vast real estate holdings in and around Ojai. Ben took one look at the purposeful look in his uncle's eyes, uttered a silent prayer and rose to greet him.

"Believe it or not, Uncle Joseph, I was just thinking about you."

"Glad to hear it, my boy. I've been thinking about you, too." He tossed the folded newspaper on to Ben's desk. "I knew it was long past time for you to get married again," his uncle commented dryly, "but did you have to keep your engagement a secret?"

Ben laughed. He hoped the laugh didn't sound as hollow to his uncle as it did to him. "Guess you could say it happened before I knew it myself."

"You don't say?" His uncle dropped into a chair, crossed his legs and looked more serious than ever. A signal that trouble was coming if there ever was one. "I wonder if the story I heard at the country club this morning could also be true?"

Ben's heart began to race. He glanced at the newspaper. Since the wedding announcement didn't seem to have shaken his uncle, there had to be something else bothering him. "What story was that, sir?"

The answer was swift and succinct. "I find it difficult to believe, but I was told your photograph appears on an Internet Web site dating service."

Confronted by the hole someone had dug for him, Ben froze. He'd been right. It *had* been too late. How in the hell was he supposed to explain what was, according to Melinda, unexplainable?

His uncle went on. "I can see from your reaction the story is true. Do you mind telling me why, if you knew Melinda Carey well enough to ask her to marry you, why you were appearing on a dating service Web site?" While Ben searched for an plausible answer, any answer, his uncle continued. "Unless, of course, that was how the two of you met?"

"Not exactly, sir. That is, the photograph is a mistake!"

"I would hope so. And the wedding announcement? Is that a mistake, too?"

"No." From the set look on his uncle's face, Ben

knew better than to confess he was having second thoughts about marrying Melinda. Or to announce the wedding might still be in an iffy stage. "It's a long story, sir, but you'll have to trust me. I believe the photograph on the Internet was intended as a joke. I've taken steps to rectify it. You have my word."

"Good, the sooner the better." His uncle motioned to the newspaper, folded open to the society section. "I'm glad to see you're marrying Bertie Blanchard's niece. Good family, good stock. Although Ms. Bertie tends to sometimes sound a little unconventional."

Ben thought of fate and destiny. "Unconventional" was being polite. "You know the lady?"

"Who doesn't?" his uncle replied. His expression softened, a smile crinkled at the corners of his eyes. "She's a fine, highly respected woman. I knew her years ago and I have a great deal of admiration for her now. You could do a lot worse than marry her niece."

Relieved, Ben mentally crossed his fingers and prayed his uncle would never get wind of the truth. "Glad you feel that way. Did you come to congratulate me, or did you have something else on your mind besides the photograph?"

Ben searched his conscience when his uncle nodded. Outside of Melinda and her fantasy wedding, he was clean.

"Yes to both questions. As a matter of fact, I'd been meaning to talk to you soon."

"About?"

"The future of the ranch and the distillery." His uncle's thoughtful gaze rested on Ben.

Relieved at the change in subject, Ben pushed the newspaper aside. "Sure. The orchards are in fine shape; producing healthy fruit right on schedule. What we haven't raised, we've imported. The distillery and its crew are doing great, too. In fact, the last batches of fruit brandies we bottled were perfect."

His uncle steepled his hands and continued to study Ben. "As is the family reputation, my boy."

Ben stirred uneasily. The message was clear; he was expected to keep that reputation intact. And he would—that is, *if* he could with Melinda and her fantasies. "The Howard legacy and reputation are just as dear to me as they are to you, Uncle Joseph."

"Good. Then we understand each other. Simply put," his uncle went on, "you might be interested to know I've been considering retiring soon. I'd planned on gifting you with the ranch the day you married. The distillery, too, if you wanted to keep it going." His uncle paused to let the importance of his announcement sink in. "I was just about to give up on you and make other plans when I saw the wedding announcement in this morning's paper." He fixed Ben with a telling stare.

Ben tried a smile. He was afraid to ask just what his uncle had intended to do with the properties if Melinda hadn't put her fantasy wedding into motion. His uncle's announcement might have come as a surprise, but Ben was in no condition to inquire what alternative his uncle had had in mind. On the other hand, maybe the announcement was a ploy to move Ben in the direction his uncle wanted. Either way, it was sink or swim. "No problem, Uncle Joseph."

A childless widower, his uncle had helped finance Ben's education. After graduation from grad school, he'd invited him to return to Ojai to help manage the Howard ranch and fruit orchards. With the vast ranch practically running itself, Ben had suggested and started a new gourmet fruit brandy distillery as a sideline. Both the ranch and the distillery had prospered. So if it wasn't money his uncle was referring to, maybe it *was* time to face up to what he owed to the family legacy.

Come hell or high water, he intended to keep that legacy proud and intact. But what he wanted most of all was his uncle's respect. He didn't have a choice, Melinda had made up his mind for him. His unexplainable decision to marry her would answer one of his uncle's concerns—the family's reputation. Married, the future of its real estate holdings would be taken care of rather than be sold to some stranger.

One thought led to another. After all, he and Melinda had a lot in common. Each of them had bonded with a close relative other than their parents. He didn't know where Melinda's folks were, but his had been lost forever on a holiday during an unexpected Caribbean hurricane. Whatever he was was due to his uncle's devotion. He owed him more than money could repay. It was pay-up time.

As for Melinda... Whatever was the basis for her close relationship with her aunt, it was touching and real. The two appeared to be harmless romantics. At least, they had been until now. To make them the laughing stock of Ojai was out of the question.

Another reason he had to go through with the make-believe marriage.

"And the photograph on the Internet, Benjamin? You won't forget to take care of that right away?"

Of course, the photograph on the Internet! Ben didn't intend to give up until he found the culprit. If Melinda wasn't behind it, someone was. And that someone was going to answer to him.

"Look, Uncle Joseph. I've told you that photograph has to be someone's idea of a joke. I don't want to sound like a conceited ass, but you know me well enough to know I don't need to advertise to find a date!"

"True," his uncle agreed with a faint smile. "You do have quite a reputation where the ladies are concerned. In fact, I've known about it for too long a time." His smile faded. "All the more reason for you to settle down, accept your responsibilities. Starting the distillery is fine, but it's time to get on with marrying again. Don't forget, it's up to you to carry on the Howard name."

Children! Ben's blood ran cold. Being tricked into marriage and going along with it for everyone else's sake was bad enough, but kids? "Sorry, sir. I can't promise you children, but at least I can provide you with a niece."

"Good enough, for now." His uncle winked. "We'll let nature take its course."

Ben mustered a feeble grin. If his uncle only knew the truth, that he'd agreed to go through a make-believe wedding, but that was as far as he intended to go. Children were out.

"Anything else on your mind, Uncle Joseph?"

"Not at the moment." His uncle rose to leave. "I'm sure I've left you with enough to think about. Just make sure you're on time for the wedding, my boy. I'll see you there."

Undecided if his uncle's departing shot was a promise or a threat, Ben shook his uncle's hand. Now, the next problem was to convince Melinda she wanted to marry him.

"MELINDA, DEAR, are you sure you feel well?"

Melinda tore her gaze from the window that looked out over the park. "Yes, I'm fine. Why do you ask?"

"You look as if you have something on your mind." Her aunt gazed lovingly at her. "But then, I suppose all young women do when they're in love and about to get married."

Melinda noticed her aunt's wistful smile. "Have you ever been in love, Aunt Bertie?"

"Yes, years ago, but I'm afraid it was one-sided. When it came down to getting married, it seemed I was the only one in love."

Melinda threw her arms around her aunt. "I'm so sorry. Whoever the man was, he missed out on getting the best and the most generous woman in the world for a wife. You would have made a wonderful wife and an even more wonderful mother."

Her aunt returned her hug. "Thank you, dear. But it wasn't as bad as all that. When you lost your mother as a little girl and came to live with me, I couldn't have asked for a more loving child than you. I'm afraid this might sound a bit selfish, but I've always thought of you as my own daughter."

"Me, too," Melinda confided with a kiss on her aunt's cheek. But instead of being happy, she was filled with guilt.

Before her aunt had interrupted her musings a few moments ago, she'd come to the conclusion the right thing to do was to release Ben from his agreement. She didn't want an "agreement," or a life filled with regret. She didn't want to burn any bridges behind her, either. Not when she still yearned for a real marriage with a man who loved her. And children while there was still time.

"And now your Benjamin will be part of my family, too," her aunt went on happily as she turned away to right a lopsided veil on a mannequin. "And one day, if the good Lord wills, there will be your children to love." She glanced back at Melinda. "I must be the luckiest woman in the world."

Melinda watched her aunt flutter around the room, straightening a box here, a counter display there. If marrying Ben was the answer to keeping the smile on her aunt's face, she couldn't broadcast her uncertainty about going through with the wedding. Make-believe or not.

Could she break her aunt's heart by backing out of the wedding now?

Melinda grabbed a light sweatshirt to cover her blue T-shirt and shorts, changed into running shoes and headed for the park across the street. A lengthy jog was just what she needed to clear her head.

She ran past the bench in front of the white lattice-wood gazebo where she'd spun countless dreams about her own wedding. Considering the disaster she'd managed to create, she should have been smart enough to confine her daydreaming to the park instead of the Internet.

The picturesque park and its story-book setting had always soothed her, but not today. The faint scent of pink climbing Cecile Brunner roses that wound their way through the gazebo's latticework wasn't working its magic. The mating calls of resident birds nesting in the trees didn't help, either. Nor did the small boy "fishing" with a fallen tree twig in the bubbling brook that ran through the park.

She'd managed to hold up well enough, but it was the sound of the boy's laughter that finally broke down her defenses. Tears came to her eyes.

She'd thought of children as she'd dreamed her wedding fantasy. Three, at the last count. Two little girls and an older brother to watch over them. The boy would have inherited his father's chiseled good looks and his legendary athletic powers. The girls, his softer image. To ensure the children could live in the daunting millennium and still be able to laugh like the little fisherman, she'd mentally added her Aunt Bertie's fey charm and her optimistic way of looking at life to the mental picture.

*How could such a harmless fantasy have become
the first steps on the road to disaster?* she wondered
as she stepped up her pace.

It wasn't as if she hadn't come close to marriage
once before. But the "something" that had stopped
her from making a final commitment had been the
same "something" vibes that had brought her back
to the small town of Ojai to check on her aunt.

Instead of finding her aunt despondent over her financial affairs, Melinda had discovered the once-
thriving shop had become more than a mere business
to Bertie. It hadn't taken Melinda long to gather that
her aunt's apparent mission was to send countless
brides happily into the future without financial hard-
ship.

In retrospect, coming home to Ojai single and alone
had been a good thing for both her and her aunt.

"Melinda! Hold up there!"

Ben Howard's voice was the last voice she wanted
to hear. She glanced over her shoulder to see him
jogging after her. In casual khaki slacks and white
knit shirt, he still resembled the boy she'd silently
admired in high school. A little older and more ma-
ture, sure, but every bit a man who sent her hormones
humming. Her heartbeat, already pounding from the
exercise, pounded faster.

She picked up her pace.

She didn't have a chance. Not when he ran beside
her as if he could run forever. She took a deep breath
and tried to get her second wind. "What's up?"

He cleared his throat. "I was driving by and decided to join you."

"You *want* to go jogging?" She didn't believe it for a minute.

"Actually, I stopped by to see if you've taken my photograph off the dating Web site."

She shook her head. "No time," she puffed. "Can't seem to get away from the telephone."

"Ditto. But I wanted to talk to you."

She didn't like the way he sounded. Ben had something on his mind. Well, so did she. And she wasn't betting on a good reaction.

"No one answered your doorbell," he went on before she started in, "so when I saw you here I figured I'd join you. So, are you getting anywhere?"

Melinda swallowed a groan. A reminder of his photograph on the Internet was the last thing she needed to worry about when she was so preoccupied with her doubts about marrying him. Even jogging wasn't helping.

"No, and Rome wasn't built in a day, either. I didn't put it on the Internet, and I'm not sure how to get it off. You'll just have to wait."

His stride paced hers. "You have no idea how many people have congratulated me over this marriage. Nor how many strange looks I got at work today. Everyone probably knows about that damn photograph. When I find out who put it there, someone's going to pay."

Melinda briefly thought of Bertie, then shrugged away the thought. Her aunt had a sixth sense, but surely she didn't have *that* kind of power. As for knowing about an Internet Web site, her aunt didn't even have a nodding acquaintance with a computer.

Taking short breaths, Melinda gazed around the park and unhappily envisioned the changes that were bound to come with the wedding. "It's a good thing you came by. I've had some second thoughts about the wedding. The truth is, I don't think we should go through with it."

He almost broke his stride. He'd sensed she was wavering, but canceling the wedding? "You're joking!"

"I'm not," she answered between puffs. "Besides, I haven't had time to get a permit to hold the wedding out here anyway. There's still time to call the whole thing off." She jogged on ahead.

Ben stepped up his pace. He grabbed her by her arm and pulled her to a stop. "No way! The announcement is in the newspaper. It's too late."

She shrugged helplessly. "It's never too late to stop a runaway train. And that's how this marriage is beginning to look to me."

"What about the reason you gave me for going along with the wedding?"

"If you mean my aunt," she muttered raggedly, "I'm sure I can come up with something."

"Like hell you will!" He turned her around to look at him. "What's the real reason?" She didn't like the fire that had come into his eyes.

She squirmed. "I just don't think it's a good idea. It's not as if you *want* to marry me."

"Not really," he agreed. "But something has come up."

"Like what?"

"We can talk about it later. And as for a license to hold the wedding in the park, I'll take care of it. Anything else?"

"Given time," she muttered, lengthening her stride, "I'm sure I can come up with something."

"Another computer fantasy?"

Melinda swung around, ready to defend herself. "That shows just how little you know about me. I'm not a dreamer—not where it counts, anyway. I was an account executive for a well-known advertising firm before I gave it up to come back here to help my aunt."

"Sure," he agreed, "and that's exactly what we're going to do...help your aunt." He drew her over to a bench. "Here, let's sit down and talk where there won't be any interruptions."

He waited until he was sure she wouldn't run, but she still looked as if she didn't know what he might do next. He didn't really blame her, he wasn't sure of himself anymore, either. "I know how much your aunt means to you. I've got good reasons for going through with the wedding myself. I'm not about to back out now." He tried to ignore the uncertain look on Melinda's face. "I think we can make this thing work if we try—for both our sakes."

Melinda was miserable. Ben was more right than wrong. Her initial reason for asking him to go along with her fantasy hadn't changed. "You could be right."

"I am," Ben said firmly. "But I hope that from now on you save your dreams for bedtime. The rest of us have to be practical."

"Practical?" She sniffed her disdain. "Don't you mean cynical?"

"If you mean that I don't believe everything I read and only half of what I see, you may be right." He leaned back against the white iron bench. "I've gotten this far by being pragmatic. I'm not about to change."

"You don't know what you're missing. Make-believe is part of life."

Ben was intrigued by the way Melinda's eyes lit up. *He* hadn't played at make-believe since he was a nine-year-old Batman. "Such as?"

"This park." She gestured to their surroundings.

"Come on," he laughed. It's only grass, flowers, a few trees and a brook."

"No wonder you don't believe in dreams." She gazed over at the meandering brook. "See the little boy over there?"

Ben followed her gesture to where a small boy was leaning over the edge of the brook. "The kid who's playing in the water?"

When he noticed the boy's mother bending over a flowering rose bush, he started to get to his feet. "What the hell. The kid's mother is smelling the roses—and he could fall in any minute!"

"That's not the point I'm trying to make. He thinks

he's fishing, and that's what counts. There!'' she added when the boy held up his twig, jumped up and down and whooped his delight. His mother smiled her approval. ''See, he's pretending he caught a fish!''

Ben brushed away a leaf that blew onto his eyes. ''Pretending might be okay for kids. The last time I looked in the mirror, I was all grown up.''

Melinda took in all six feet of Ben. The faint scent of shaving lotion, wavy brown hair and timeless blue eyes. With his muscular arms and a chest that tapered to a narrow waist, he was more attractive now than as a teenage basketball hero and definitely grown up. She felt herself blush.

The arm that brushed hers in passing was all grown up, too.

She remembered the first time she'd become aware of Ben, the most popular boy at school. She'd mooned over him the entire year. Now, it seemed not much had changed. Maybe that was why she'd picked him off the Internet?

''Childhood is when dreams begin,'' she went on, trying to put her sensuous thoughts behind her. They were a waste of time since Ben had already put her on notice that their marriage was going to be platonic. And, according to him, preferably short. ''There's time enough for reality to bite. It would be a shame if we quit dreaming just because we're not children anymore.''

''Sorry. You can dream as long as you don't include me. My own dreams, if you can call them that, were knocked out of me with my divorce. I sure as hell don't dream anymore.''

"Not even about children?"

He looked at her as if it were the first time he'd actually seen her. "What children are we talking about?"

"Forget it...it was just a thought." She looked over to where the little fisherman was skipping out of sight alongside his mother. If their marriage had had a chance of being real, she would have told Ben how much she would have liked to be his wife and have his children.

His next question almost floored her. "If you like children so much, how come you haven't gotten married by now and had a few kids of your own?"

Good question. How ironic it should have come from him, the man she'd visualized as her children's father. She wiped away a wisp of hair a gentle wind had blown across her eyes and met his gaze. "Because I've never found the right father for them." *Until now. Now, when it was too late.*

Ben stirred uneasily. "Sorry. It's none of my business."

Melinda glanced at Ben, murmured goodbye and rose to leave. Children would have been his business, if he'd wanted hers. "I'll let you know what I decide to do."

Under the circumstances, the thought that Ben would turn out to be her "husband" was enough to make her swear off ever thinking of getting married for real.

Ben watched Melinda cross the street. Her body language was telling. She not only looked miserable, he figured he was the one who had made her feel that way. He felt guilty as hell. Even a nearby weeping willow tree drooped its reproach.

His mind wandered back to the little boy in the park. The kid had been cute, sure, but as far he was concerned dreams were still for children. He was marrying Melinda for more practical reasons—he hadn't misled her about that.

Still, as she disappeared from sight, he thought Melinda was someone special. He might not have remembered her in high school, but she'd sure turned into a lovely woman. With honey-blond hair that framed suntanned features and a slender body that was womanly in all the right places, she was eye-catching. And there were her eyes—emerald eyes that reflected intelligence and compassion. Dangerous thoughts for a guy who had dedicated himself to being single.

Back to something more important than Melinda's looks—how could she still be thinking of backing out of the wedding?

Maybe it was because she didn't really know the real him. Considering how attracted he was to her, it was something he was going to have to remedy. And soon.

Chapter Four

"Lunch?"

Ben stood in the doorway. He wore khaki slacks, a light blue T-shirt that matched his eyes and a wide smile. He held a picnic hamper in one hand and looked as innocent as a newborn kitten.

Melinda knew better.

Sunday, he'd sent a dozen red roses.

Monday, he'd asked to come over and talk. She'd told him she was too busy cleaning the house and straightening up the bridal shop.

Today was Tuesday. What next?

She'd already sensed he was the type of man who acted only after a great deal of thought. After all, he was a prominent businessman and had a reputation as a philanthropist who supported children's sports and the high school's basketball team. A man who had that kind of reputation looked before he leaped. Maybe that was why he hadn't been able to make up his mind about their fantasy wedding. What was he up to?

Still, a picnic seemed harmless enough. Except...

She glanced over his shoulder at the little park where she'd spent so many happy hours. A picnic in that magical place was out. A man who didn't appreciate the park's special charm didn't belong there.

"What did you have in mind?" She couldn't keep her suspicions of him out of her mind.

He spread his arms wide as if to show her he was harmless. "Just a picnic. You look dressed for one."

Melinda looked down at her short cotton sundress with its slender spaghetti straps. A dress that had seemed perfectly proper an hour ago left her feeling exposed.

"Why a picnic?"

Taken aback by her blunt question, he blinked. "You have to have a reason for a picnic?"

She nodded and squirmed to bring her neckline higher. "In this case, yes."

He looked puzzled. "I thought a picnic is the sort of thing engaged couples do—spend time together. I figured it would give us a chance to get to know each other before the wedding."

He was back to talking about a wedding she'd already told him she wasn't sure she wanted any part of! "I haven't made up my mind about the wedding, remember?" she reminded him. "And until I do, we are *not* engaged."

"We're not? Funny, everyone seems to think we are."

"I don't."

"Aren't two people about to get married considered engaged?" Before she could answer, he reached for her left hand and studied her bare ring finger. "Maybe I should have gotten you an engagement ring to convince you."

Melinda drew a deep breath. The man had a one-track mind and maybe a deaf ear! She was about to tell him her opinion of engagements and engagement rings, when the raucous sound of an automobile horn drowned out her reply.

"Congratulations you two! Stay cool!" Melinda's friend, Mary Olsen, shouted out the car window as she slowly drove by. "Save it for after the wedding!"

To Melinda's chagrin, two Ojai Valley Nursery delivery men parked across the street straightened up at the sound of the horn. They laughed. She didn't. One man cheerfully motioned to the flowering white gardenia plants they were unloading and pointed to her. Clearly, they'd begun to ready the park for her wedding. Dollar signs danced in front of her eyes as she envisioned the bills about to come through the mail—or the penalties if she canceled the wedding. She was going to get a bill no matter which way she chose to go.

She snatched back her hand and motioned Ben into the house. "Come on in before you make a bigger public spectacle out of this than you already have."

He cheerfully followed her into the house. "Does that mean you've decided to come with me?"

She closed the door behind him with a bang. With the bridal shop just off Ojai's Main Street, Mary wouldn't have been the only one to see Ben holding her hand. "No," she answered firmly. "I'm still thinking."

"How about for old times' sake?" His crooked smile teased and did a number on her. Only a stone could have resisted that smile. But she wasn't ready to give in. Not yet, anyway.

"There weren't any old times, Ben Howard!" she sniffed. "You said yourself you didn't remember me."

"True, but you remember me, right?"

Melinda nodded reluctantly. She remembered him a lot more than she was comfortable with. Why else would she have picked him off the dating Web site? Or be standing here arguing about being engaged.

"How about if we say I'm trying to make up for lost time?" The killer smile on his face sent a sensuous current coursing through her. And cracked the wall she'd woven around her heart.

Not even her former fiancé had managed to ignite the erotic response in her Ben managed to do with a single smile. More interested in having her work for him than having her for his wife, Paul's kisses had been practiced, his glances remote and his commitment to a wedding date vague. She'd lived on promises until she given him back an engagement ring whose diamond looked as cold as his heart.

She'd wanted a man who saw her as a woman and not only as a role she represented in his life. Paul hadn't even bothered to get to know the woman in her. And now there was Ben, insisting they were engaged, but who didn't know her at all.

So why was a warmth coursing through her at his smile? What would she do if he actually made a pass at her?

She stirred uneasily. The expression he wore was so earnest, she could have believed he was sincere about wanting to be engaged and eventually married. Except that she knew better.

There was a problem. He'd been sending mixed messages for a week. For a man who had demanded a platonic and even a temporary marriage, he was going about persuading her he wanted to go through with her fantasy in the wrong way.

To begin with, there was that seductive smile that tugged at her heart. And the way her senses reacted when he took her hand in his. His firm, vibrant grip was that of a man who knew what he wanted. And it looked as if he wanted her!

A picnic with just the two of them was dangerous.

Who knew what might happen on a secluded picnic with a man she was so attracted to? Who knew what he had in mind besides lunch? And who knew how she would react?

For her sake, as well as his, it was time to put her cards on the table. If Ben wanted a platonic relationship, she intended to give it to him. But not before making herself clear.

"Okay, I'll go. But before I do, I want it understood that it's just going to be conversation. No touching."

He pretended innocence. "I don't remember suggesting anything else. As long as I seem to be on probation, I'll try to concentrate on just being friendly.''

''Friendly, my eye,'' she muttered. She'd been around men enough to recognize an attempted seduction of the senses when she saw it.

She was tempted to tell him what she thought of his sensuous smile and the invitation in his voice. Let alone the blatant challenge reflected in his eyes. How he'd managed to remain single with a persona like his was a mystery.

''You'll have to wait until my aunt comes back. I'd hate to close the shop.''

''How about giving yourself a break and living it up today?'' he coaxed with a twinkle in his eyes. ''Hang a Closed sign on the door. From what your aunt told me, no one is going to break down the door trying to buy a wedding dress. They can come back.''

The reminder that the shop's financial balance was dripping with red ink was bad enough. Did he have to rub it in?

''A closed door isn't an invitation to potential business. As a businessman, you ought to know that.''

''Right,'' he agreed, ''but you can't be in two places at one time. We'll have more privacy where I intend to take you. I figured you wanted to talk.''

Melinda bit her lower lip and calculated the possibility of someone dropping by to order a wedding dress. Ben was right. ''I need to change.''

''What's the matter with what you're wearing?''

From his point of view, there was obviously nothing wrong with her skimpy summer dress. From hers, she clearly needed some armor. She settled for a jacket.

"By the way, my uncle tells me the groom is supposed to furnish the drinks at his wedding reception. Just tell me what you'd like, and I'll have it sent over."

Melinda's patience reached the end of the line. "That won't be necessary! I keep telling you I'm still not sure there *is* going to be a wedding, let alone a reception!"

"All the greater reason for us to talk." He strode to the door and turned the Open sign around. "Leave a note for your aunt and let's go."

IN FULL VIEW of shopkeepers, interested local spectators and the usual influx of summer tourists, Ben drove through the three blocks of Ojai's Main Street. The top of his convertible was down. By the time he reached the other end of town, everyone who counted had a chance to get a good look at Melinda. Now let her try to wiggle out of the wedding! He whistled contentedly while Melinda tried to make herself invisible.

She didn't have a chance. In her brief dress, whose spaghetti straps didn't look strong enough for the job of covering her lovely breasts, it was an impossible dream. Even he couldn't keep his eyes off her.

It was a perfect June day. With the early morning haze that drifted off of the ocean gone, the sun was shining its heart out. The scent of orange blossoms filled the air. Tourists strolled under the arches that covered the sidewalks. He was filled with a sense of well-being as he drove past acres of orange trees. They passed horse ranches and an occasional rambling ranch house. His own home sat high in the hills that bordered the valley.

He cast an occasional glance at his silent companion. The breeze ruffled the blond hair his fingers itched to touch, to smooth. She was beginning to relax. Her mouth parted in a smile that hovered at the corner of her lips. She hadn't said much since they'd left the bridal shop, but he was beginning to have high hopes. Maybe she realized how compatible they could be. "You're awfully quiet. Sorry you came along?"

"Not at all." Her contended smile touched a part of him he didn't know still existed. "How could I be sorry? I missed all of this during the years I lived in San Francisco."

"You must have come back occasionally to see your aunt," he commented. And why hadn't he noticed her when she did? Of course, he thought with a wry smile, a bridal shop would have been the last place he would have visited.

"Not as often as I liked. First there was college and then a job. Something seemed to come up every time I planned to come home." She turned her face up to his and smiled. "This time, I'm here to stay."

He felt relieved. He would have hated to see her leave.

"Great. But what are you going to do if Ms. Bertie's shop folds?"

"Don't even think about it!" She looked horrified.

"As long as my aunt wants to keep the shop open, I'm not going to let it close. Not if I can help it!"

Gazing at the resolute look on her face, he was ready to believe it. "How are you going to do that?"

She shrugged. "I have some money I've saved. When that's gone, I can always get a job."

Ben took his eyes off the road long enough to glance at her set lips and eyes that glinted with determination. He was tempted to lean over and kiss those lips until they parted under his. He wasn't sure where the thought came from, but he put it down to the fragrant scent of the orange blossoms. It was turning his good intentions to mush. The truth was he'd wanted to kiss Melinda almost from the first moment he'd stormed the bridal shop.

He couldn't understand his reaction to Melinda. She had become a puzzle he wanted to solve. It wasn't as if he hadn't had a few relationships after his impetuous marriage and subsequent divorce, but none that had lasted. As for Melinda, he'd only known her for a few short days, but he found himself dwelling on a future with her.

His thoughts were in a turmoil. What was there about Melinda that had gotten to him so quickly. Why was he going along with a fantasy that had an uncertain future?

She was attractive, sure, but not cover-girl attractive. She had spunk and imagination that lent her a special quality, but he'd met women like her before and passed them by. So why Melinda?

A bigger puzzlement: why was his mind focused on kissing the last woman who wanted his kisses?

He turned his attention to the narrow two-lane road that wound its way up through the foothills surrounding the Ojai valley. True to form, his heartbeat picked up in the anticipation of seeing the fruit orchards and the micro distillery that was his baby, his pride and joy. And the opportunity to show it to Melinda.

He felt lucky. He'd started the distillery to have a purpose. Certainly not for the money it would bring. When it came to brass tacks, there would always be a place for him somewhere in the Howard enterprises. And a salary that would come with the job.

It wasn't the same for Melinda. As far as he could tell, she was working her heart out without a chance of making it.

If her love and loyalty to her aunt hadn't stood in the way, she was obviously smart enough to know when to quit. Instead, she had the bridal shop hanging around her neck like an albatross.

Since she couldn't seem to help herself, all the more reason he had to help her.

The country club where he was a member was full of eligible women. He could ask Josie Morrison, his best friend's wife, to drop a discreet word or two there about the beautiful gowns at Bertie's Bridal shop. Or even mention how helpful Melinda's bridal referral service would be for a bride in need of advice. Of course, Melinda would have to give up daydreaming on the Internet, or there'd be hell to pay. Their own approaching wedding was a case in point.

Providing he could persuade her to go along with it, the game they were playing was funny, if not interesting, he mused with a sidelong glance at Melinda. When she'd suggested he go along with her fantasy, he'd said no. And now that he'd convinced himself they both needed to go along with the wedding, she was saying no! It sounded like a romantic comedy plot, except it didn't look as if they were going to have a happy ending.

He turned into the parking lot. On the right, there was the distillery with a sign above the door, Oak Tree Distillery, Ben Howard, Proprietor. On the left, an old picnic table was shaded by a large oak tree and a small patch of grass perfect for what he had in mind.

The picnic would have to wait. In case that was what was bugging her, he wanted to show her he wasn't just a playboy. He wanted to show off the distillery that had been his idea from start to finish. "How about a tour of the distillery before lunch?"

She looked doubtful. "Aren't they working in there?"

"Not at the moment. The apricots and peaches aren't ripe yet. It's vacation time for the brewers. We'll be alone."

Alone! Melinda swallowed a comment. Instead, she turned to admire the building and the sign above the door. "I understood you started the distillery a few years ago—it looks as if it's been here forever."

"Close enough. It was part of an earlier operation, until the previous owners moved up north and my uncle bought the property. Come on in, I'll show you around. I have some Evian water cooling on ice inside.''

''No brandy?''

''No.'' He grinned. ''I want you sober when I...''

Melinda halted in mid stride. ''When you what?''

Ben's smile faded at the foreboding tone in her voice. ''I just meant I wanted us to be able to talk, to get acquainted.''

''And I have to be sober to talk?''

''Preferably,'' he answered with a wicked grin. ''I didn't want you to think I was taking advantage of you.''

''That'll be the day,'' she rejoined, mollified for the moment. She took a deep breath as they walked inside the building. The scent of fruit mixed with alcohol was intoxicating. For a moment, she wondered what the fruit brandy would taste like. Too bad she didn't drink. ''Lead on.''

He showed her around the small distillery where apricots and peaches had been simmered and set to ferment in wooden casks. Six large oak barrels lined the center of the room. The scent of fermented fruit hung in the air. He took a deep breath and smiled. ''Great, isn't it?''

Melinda gazed around her at the peaceful and cool setting. ''It's kind of small. Are you sure it's for real?''

''It is. The bottling operation is done elsewhere. But on the other hand the prices we get for our fruit brandy is right.''

Melinda paused in front of a small fire that glowed. "You actually cook the fruit?"

"Yes, and then we let it ferment. The process goes this way: water is distilled from the fermented fruit, sometimes two or three times. What remains is infused with alcohol and becomes fruit brandy. It's stored for six weeks in wood casks to give it a flavor and aged for two years in those large wooden barrels. It's a slow process that's been around for hundreds of years, but it sure pays off. Especially when we're one of only two brandy distilleries in California."

Melinda gazed around her. "You sound as if you love the business."

"Yes, I do. It's a heck of a lot more rewarding than any other thing I've ever done." He paused beside a small sampling cask, his hand on the spigot. "Want a taste?"

Melinda started to shake her head, then took the small glass he handed her. She'd learned the hard way that whenever she took a drink she became sleepy. And sleepy was the last thing she wanted to be around Ben. She had a few things to settle with him before they parted for good. On the other hand, how much damage could one little drink do?

Ben took a bottle of Evian from an ice-filled champagne bucket, dried it off and stuck it in his pocket.

Melinda wasn't fooled. From the too casual sound of his voice, she was sure he intended to persuade her to go through with the wedding. He was in for a surprise. "Outside of the wedding, just what was it you wanted to talk about?"

"Don't be so suspicious," he chided. "You seem to know all about me. If we're going to be married, it's only fair for me to know something about you."

She shrugged. "That's only because you were Ojai's star athlete. My autobiography is short. I was born in Santa Barbara and lived there until I was eight. My mother died about then, and I was sent to live with my aunt. After high school, I went to college in San Francisco and worked there until I came back to help my aunt. End of story."

"Your father?"

She was tempted to say her father was a man who didn't care enough to want to know her, to stick around, but she settled for a brief comment. "He was a child-support check for a few years. After that, nothing. I don't know what would have become of me if it hadn't been for my aunt. I love her very much and owe her more than money can repay."

"Maybe we're more alike than you know."

Melinda swallowed her reply. Unlike was more like it. She was an average woman with a large responsibility, and no money. With his athletic good looks, self-confidence and reputation as a ladies' man, Ben was a great deal more than an average man. If he had responsibilities, at least he had the money to pay for them. How alike could they be?

He led the way to the picnic table. "Ready for lunch?"

"Yes. But first, I'd like to know why you came back and agreed to go along with me after you'd just finished storming out of the shop. And don't tell me it's because of what my aunt told you about her finances.''

She went on before he could answer. "It seems to me no man gives up his freedom easily when he's spent ten years trying so hard to preserve it.'' She regarded him suspiciously. "You might as well stick to facts.''

"Sure. I intended to.'' He unpacked the picnic basket and set out a small tablecloth. He pulled out a dried Italian sausage, a container of pickles and olives and the utensils to go with them. Next came two oranges. She hid a smile at a man's idea of a picnic.

She stopped smiling when he told her about the bargain he'd struck with his uncle. Of all the reasons he could have had to want to go through with her fantasy, this was the last one she'd thought of.

"You want to go through with the marriage to keep the distillery? You've got to be kidding!''

"You've got it wrong! I want to get married for my uncle's sake. I wouldn't want to disappoint him. The distillery has nothing to do with it. I owe him every bit as much as you say you owe Ms. Bertie. And for much the same reasons.''

Melinda was so disgusted, she was ready to turn on her heel and hike down the hill. And to hike all the way back to Ojai before she'd let him drive her there.

"Was your conversation with your uncle before or after you agreed to go through with the fantasy marriage?'' After her earlier unhappy engagement in San

Francisco, how could she have not known Ben was just another man who was using her for his own ends.

He crossed his heart, a baguette of French bread in his hand. "After. I swear."

He looked so comical waving the loaf of bread in the air, Melinda would have laughed if she hadn't felt she was being used. "Why me? You don't even know me, let alone like me!"

"That's where you're wrong. I like you all right." He dropped the baguette in to the picnic basket, grabbed her and proceeded to kiss her senseless.

Instinctively, Melinda leaned into the kiss she'd dreamed of for years. First as a high school girl, then as a grown woman. She closed her eyes and wrapped her arms around his neck and lived her dream. He tasted of apricot brandy and desire. A desire that matched hers in its fury.

When his lips urged hers to part, she found herself more than willing. The doubts and fears of the unexpected events of the past weeks began to fade. Whatever Ben intended it to be, his kiss was no dream. The kiss was real, and for now she intended to enjoy it.

She parted her lips—their tongues met. Threads of electrical currents shot through her. Lost in a haze of desire, she reached to touch, to caress, the tanned skin at his open collar. To finger the bronze hair that curled at the nape of his neck. To live out her dream.

His kiss deepened. His arms tightened around her until she could feel his arousal. A voice whispered: *Stop before it's too late!*

She couldn't. Not when she was living her wildest dreams. Not when her fantasies appeared to be on the verge of becoming true. And yet, she hesitated at the brink of fulfilling desire.

"Melinda? Is something wrong?"

She hesitated before she shook her head and put a finger to his lips. "No. For a moment, I was afraid this was only a dream and I would wake up." She smiled shyly. "If this is a dream, I don't want it to end."

"I don't want this to end, either." He wanted to taste, to touch, to fulfill the longing to make her his. His heart pounded, rational thought along with any earlier reluctance to enter a relationship with Melinda, disappeared. He slowly swept her body with his hands, felt the womanly curves he admired from the first moment they'd met. When she didn't draw away, he cupped her breasts with his hands, gently brushing their tips with his thumbs.

And yet, even as he thrilled to hear her low murmur of arousal and the echoing sensations that swept over him, he recalled Melinda's slight hesitation a moment ago. He'd been sure she was going to tell him to stop. Instead, she'd pressed closer until his kisses had deepened.

What had she been thinking? What had she wanted to say before he took her lips back in his? His conscience stirred. Doubts and questions roiled through his mind.

The unusual relationship he was contemplating

with Melinda was going to be platonic and short, wasn't it?

The marriage was a concession to satisfy his uncle and help Ms. Bertie, wasn't it?

Under the circumstances, did he have the right to touch Melinda like this, to make love to her?

And if he did, would Melinda understand their fantasy wedding wouldn't end in a lasting relationship, let alone marriage?

His arousal was sheer torture. He wanted Melinda more than any woman he'd wanted before. He glanced at the secluded grassy area under the trees where he could make love to her. As for what tomorrow would bring, as long as Melinda seemed willing to live for the moment, he was prepared to let tomorrow take care of itself.

"Ben?" There was that hesitancy again. He looked down into the depths of green eyes wide with unasked questions. He slackened his embrace when he sensed they were questions for which he had no ready answers. She wanted some reassurance from him that he cared for her, that this was real. And for promises he couldn't keep.

She looked so vulnerable, so lost in a romantic haze, his conscience took over. Until he had the answers to his own questions about the future, how could he answer hers? He shook his head. It was the only answer he could give her.

Melinda's heartbeat slowed to normal. Her gaze locked with Ben's. His lips were set in a grim line, the expression in his eyes filled with regret. From his still obvious arousal, there was no doubt that he wanted her.

Alarm bells rang. Women were free to love as they wanted, but how could she make love when she was the only one in love? She wasn't a child anymore, nor did she believe in fairy tales.

She was tempted, so tempted to let him make love to her. To live the dream she'd carried with her through the years.

Until she realized that although Ben was the man she wanted, he was also the man who wanted her for all the wrong reasons.

She pulled out of his embrace. "Maybe we should just talk, after all."

Chapter Five

His eyebrows rose at an angle Melinda now knew spelled trouble. He shot her an ironic look. "Okay, maybe we *should* talk first."

She read his mind as easily as his expression. Talking was the last thing he had in mind. She also knew men didn't like to be teased. And she was sure he thought she'd been toying with him. If he only knew, pulling out of his embrace hadn't come easily.

She didn't really know Ben. Who was this stranger with inviting lips, an obstinate chin and bedroom eyes? Just looking at him had her yearning to be back in his arms and loved, if only for a little while.

Her senses still throbbing with desire, Melinda sat on the picnic bench. She wanted to keep a safe distance between them, but her senses told her no distance was enough to keep her from responding to the invitation in his eyes. Her nipples were hard from his touch, her body ached to have his strong arms around her still. She'd had to stop herself from making a mistake. She had to face the truth and make Ben face it with her. They were two people who had nothing in common but physical desire.

"Ben…"

He held a warning finger to her lips. "On the other hand, let's not talk. Don't spoil what we have going between us."

"That's the point. What's going on between us is pure biology, nothing else."

"Biology is fine with me," he said, flashing a wicked grin.

"Not for me," she replied succinctly. "I've been there and it isn't enough. There has to be more than a physical attraction. You really didn't want *me*. I could have been any woman."

"Strange, I thought we were doing great." He walked a few steps away. Over his shoulder, he said, "Excuse me a minute while I imagine icebergs and cold showers and hard-hearted women."

His effort to calm himself was so evident she ached. Both for him and for herself. Every nerve in her body cried for what might have been.

"Give me a break," she said, leaping to her feet and moving to his side. Hesitantly, she touched his arm. "I'm not made of stone, Ben. I hate this as much as you do."

"You could have fooled me."

She tried to ignore his cut, but it still hurt. "Listen to me, please." He turned around reluctantly. "I've always wanted to believe there is someone special out there just for me. A man who's taken the trouble to know me. A man who loves me for who I am, and not just someone who's convenient to have around."

He winced. Her verbal arrow must have found its mark. "And you've never found one?"

"I thought I had. No, it's not you," she added when a wary look passed over his face. "I was engaged to be married before I came back to live in Ojai. Until I realized what my fiancé wanted was an unpaid executive assistant with the title of a wife. It was cheaper that way." She couldn't keep her bitter memories out of her voice as she told him the whole miserable story of her failed engagement.

"That's tough," he conceded, turning his head so she saw again the neat contrast between his blue shirt and sun-warmed throat. A reluctant smile covered his face. "No other men in your life?"

She stared blindly at a hummingbird hovering over the picnic basket. Its wings fluttered wildly until it realized the tantalizing contents were out of its reach. After a frenzied series of dives, the bird flew away.

Melinda glanced up at Ben. What thoughts were flashing through those crisp blue eyes? He was out of her reach as surely as the picnic basket had been out of the hummingbird's. Maybe the man she yearned for didn't exist. If he had, she wouldn't have had to resort to fabricating a fantasy wedding on her computer. She would have been living it by now. "There weren't any other men in my life, except for my father. And he's never shown he cared about me, either."

Ben's ardor had cooled. He pulled the picnic basket toward him and began to repack their untouched lunch. A squirrel at the base of the oak tree chattered. With a wry shrug, Ben tore off a crust of bread and threw it on the grass. "Maybe you're asking for too much. From the way it sounds, you don't want a man, you want a saint."

"I don't think so," she answered quietly. "I know you think I'm a hopeless romantic, but I'm too realistic for that. Just a flesh and blood and caring man. I'm not talking about perfection," she hurried on to explain when it appeared he was going to bring up her Internet fantasy. "How could I when I'm not perfect myself? But I want the man to want *me* for *myself*. And not for someone else's sake," she added pointedly.

He studied an orange he held in his hand for a moment. Then, as if deciding something important, he tossed it into the picnic basket and closed the lid. "You are talking about me, aren't you?" She nodded. "Come on, Melinda." He went on, "You're not being fair. I was being honest when I told you my uncle wants us to get married. But it wasn't any different from your own motives. As I understand it, you needed a man for your fantasy wedding and just happened to pick me. I could have been just any man."

"That's not the way it was!"

He waved her protest. "I'm sorry if I'm not what you wanted, but I still believe we should go through with the scenario you dreamed up. You have your reasons and I have mine, so we're even. As for not getting the man you bargained for, remember that old saying, Let the Buyer Beware. As far as I'm concerned, you chose me, and I'm yours for the duration."

Melinda winced at the cynical note in his voice. It

was obvious he didn't trust her sincerity any more than she could trust his. She'd been foolish to think he was different from all the other men she'd known.

"I see only one solution to this trust question," he finally said.

"Tell me," she asked, a leap of hope brightening her eyes in spite of herself.

"I can only speak for myself, you understand. I don't even know if I can do it all the time. But I'm going to try to trust your judgment all the way."

Relieved, she started to smile. Then the implication of his wry comment hit her. "Do you know what you're saying?"

"Lord help me, I do," he said, eyeing a new resident hummingbird. "It's a first for me."

"A first what?"

"Backing off when I know how much we want each other."

She had to be content with his answer, but still an unsettling thought stuck in her mind. He might desire her, but he still didn't understand why she'd asked him to wait before they made love. Maybe men couldn't separate sexual desire from love, but she could. When she made love with him, it was going to be because he cared for her.

If he couldn't figure out that she'd chosen him out of all the available men on the dating Web site because she was halfway in love with him, nothing she could have said would have made a difference now.

"By the way," Ben went on after a moment's hesitation, "I hope you realize we're going to have to live together after the wedding. Otherwise the marriage won't look real.''

Melinda blinked. She hadn't had time to carry her Internet fantasy that far before she'd been interrupted, but Ben was right. "I'm still not sure there *is* going to be a wedding! As for living together..." Wide-eyed, she stared at him.

"Don't tell me you didn't think that far ahead when you planned this caper?"

"No, why would I have? I keep telling you I never meant to put my fantasy into action! Why would I have planned on living with you?"

"Because that's what normal, newly married people do," Ben said slowly, as if to a child. "And, sometimes when they're not married," he added with a grin as she appeared incredulous at the idea they would have to share living quarters. "You don't sound as if you have much experience with this marriage business, do you?"

"No, I haven't," she answered with a blush he thought was charming. "Paul and I hadn't managed to get that far. Not that he didn't suggest it. As time went on, the last thing I wanted to do was to live with him. I gave him my working hours, and that was enough!"

"Sounds to me as if you had a strange kind of an engagement," Ben remarked as he watched conflicting emotions pass over Melinda's face. "No wonder you're gun-shy about this marriage business."

"Not gun-shy," she replied. "Just cautious."

Ben didn't like the watchful way Melinda was sizing him up, but he forged ahead anyway. "In that case, since I do have some experience along those lines, maybe I should do the planning for the two of us."

"That depends on what you have in mind."

After he realized this was the chance to try again at convincing Melinda to marry him, he pretended to stop and think. He came up with the only logical answer in thirty seconds. "It's simple. Married people live together. How about my place? Except for my houseman, Manuel, there wouldn't be anyone there but the two of us. And, if you object to his company, I can always give him the vacation he has coming."

Melinda looked doubtful. Her bottom lip curled over the top lip a fraction of an inch in a gesture that made him want to kiss her doubts away and take up action where he'd left off. He'd promised to behave, but he couldn't resist the chance to put another blush on her face.

"I guess it would be better than our moving in with my aunt. She would be the first one to realize something was wrong. That is, if I decide to marry you."

"Living together would be wrong only if you think it is." He knew it was a mistake to try again, but he couldn't resist a nudge in the direction he was leaning. "After all, we'd be husband and wife."

"That's a technicality," she said with a cool look.

Clearly, it was up to him to make the next move now that he'd gotten her to even consider his proposition. "Why don't we go on up to my place?" he said persuasively. "You can check it out and make any changes you like before you move in. Or, if you'd rather, you can wait until after the wedding." He was counting on her female curiosity.

"And your promise—is it still good?"

Ben stilled his clamoring conscience. "Until you ask me to break it. I promise not to do anything you don't want me to do."

Melinda thought of the temptations of living in intimate quarters with Ben, even platonically. She didn't know the extent of his past love life, but she didn't want to become part of it.

Not if you can help it, a small voice whispered. She wasn't sure if she *could* help it. Not when Ben's eyes gleamed with an unvoiced invitation that had her good intentions in tatters. "If you're waiting for me to change my mind, I'm afraid you're going to wait a long time!"

He raised a quizzical eyebrow as if he knew better. His crooked grin tantalized her until she couldn't think straight. "Until you find the one guy you think is meant for you?"

"Until I find the one man who's meant for me," she echoed firmly. More for herself than him.

BEN UNLOCKED the door to his Spanish-style home high in the foothills above Ojai and ushered her inside.

"Mr. Ben." A slight figure dressed in black trousers, white shirt and black tie seemed to materialize from out of nowhere and stood waiting.

"Ah, Manuel." Ben drew Melinda to his side. "I'd like to introduce you to my fiancée, Melinda Carey. Melinda, this is the man who is in charge around here,

Manuel Torres. Manuel, you'll be happy to know Miss Carey and I are getting married in two weeks.''

Manuel smiled before she could add "Maybe." "My pleasure, Miss Carey. If there is anything I can do to make your stay enjoyable, please ask.''

"Thank you, I will.'' She watched as he glided out of sight. "Manuel sounds like a college student.''

"As a matter of fact, he is. He's been taking college extension courses through the mail.''

Melinda gazed around the impressive entryway that led into the house. The floors were laid with marble, the walls were covered with eclectic works of art. Three of the walls rose two floors above the entry before they ended in stained-glass etchings. The front wall was a series of large picture windows that looked out over the Ojai valley floor.

Large, comfortable furniture, obviously made in Mexico, filled the surrounding open area and the adjoining living room.

As if that wasn't impressive enough, Melinda found herself gazing at a graceful curved iron staircase that wound its way to a second floor.

She counted at least six areas opening off the spacious atrium that was the entry. "All of this for just one person?''

"I entertain a lot,'' Ben answered with a wry grin. "But I'm afraid it does look as if the architect and I got carried away. There's a kitchen, a dining room and service area back there,'' he gestured to his left. "And five bedrooms upstairs. Are you game for a tour of the rest of the house?''

Melinda glanced around for the houseman. "Where did Manuel go?"

Ben shrugged. "Probably to the kitchen. If I know him, he already has his own brand of iced tea waiting for us in the den. Care for a drink?"

"Yes, thank you. I'm impressed. Does he do that for all the women you bring home?"

Ben stopped in midstride, serious again. "I don't know what ideas you have about me, but no. Outside of entertaining friends and business associates, I've never brought what you politely call a "woman" here. I would never treat my home lightly."

"That makes me the first?"

"First *wife*," he corrected and led the way to the den.

In spite of her misgivings, Melinda was taken by the idea she *was* almost a wife. And to a man she'd thought of for most of her adult life. Too bad she didn't stand a chance of becoming the kind of wife she'd dreamed of being if she actually married him. "How many wives have you had?"

He glanced back over his shoulder. "Before you? Just one."

"No children?" Melinda asked, even as she pictured a little boy who looked like Ben.

"No, no children."

"You don't like children?"

"Sure I do. I wanted eight, but I've never found the time, nor the right woman."

"Eight?" she squeaked.

"Why not?" he shrugged. "They're only make-believe. You ought to understand that."

Ben poured iced tea into a tall, frosted glass and added a sprig of mint to the rim. "Lemon?" She shook her head. Ice cubes clinked as he handed her the glass.

She gazed at him over the rim of her glass. No wonder he hadn't found the right woman. The idea of eight children would have scared off the most domestic of women. Three would have been enough for her. "Aren't eight a little excessive, even if they're make-believe?"

He laughed. "You've got a point."

Melinda digested his answer as she sipped cinnamon-laced iced tea. Maybe she'd been too hasty in measuring the Ben of today against the Ben of years ago. She'd convinced herself he was a handsome rogue who, if rumors were true, had legions of women chasing after him. At least, she thought with a wry smile, until they heard about the eight babies.

She'd actually been embarrassed to think of herself becoming one of his women when she'd found his photograph on the Internet. And yet, she'd chosen him from the dating Web site just the same. At the time, she'd believed that surely no one would ever know about her foolish musings. She shuddered. Look at her now!

In hindsight, she realized she'd chosen Ben for his strong, masculine looks and the mental picture of him as a high school senior. He definitely wasn't the high school hero anymore. The grown up Ben was a decent, sensitive man whose ideas of a home and a family weren't too far apart from her own. What other surprises were there in store for her?

"Ready for a tour of the house?" She nodded. "The kitchen?"

"Er...no thanks. I'll leave that to Manuel. Frankly, I'm not much of a cook. If you get hungry, you'll have to eat out."

The look that came into his eyes told her it hadn't been her cooking skills that had been on his mind.

"The bedrooms?" He started to reach for her empty glass.

She clutched the cold glass to a heated cheek. "Bedrooms?"

"You do want to choose a bedroom for yourself, don't you? Or—" he leered playfully "—would you rather share mine?"

"Behave yourself," she hissed as she looked over her shoulder. "I'm sure Manuel can hear every word we say! What will he think?"

"Not a thing," Ben answered. "I'm sure he knows all engaged couples kid around."

"Okay, but remember. We're not engaged yet!" She handed him the glass. She'd never run away from anything before and she didn't intend to start now. "Lead on."

"Be careful," Ben cautioned as he motioned her to proceed him. "These open staircases can be a little intimidating."

Not as much as you are, Melinda thought wildly when he put his hand under her elbow to guide her up the first step. She shook off his hand and cautiously headed up the curved iron staircase.

The sight of Melinda's swaying hips as she made her way up the stairs became a definite challenge to

Ben's libido. He tried to restrain himself, to remember his promise to let her call the shots in their unusual relationship.

Relationship? Hell, he thought as he made his way up the stairs behind Melinda. The only relationship he had to look forward to was a fantasy marriage with a reluctant bride!

He wanted more. Maybe not the whole nine yards that included a real marriage, but enough to satisfy the testosterone raging inside him. He prided himself on wanting and working hard to earn the best things in life. Right now the best was Melinda. He'd take their unusual situation one day at a time. Otherwise it would be an empty victory.

He threw open the door to his bedroom. "This is my bedroom."

"Right." Melinda stood in the doorway and took a quick look at a masculine bedroom decorated in shades of gray with touches of maroon. The four-poster bed looked large enough to accommodate every one of the eight children Ben had mentioned he wanted. Matching maroon leather armchairs fronted a huge brick fireplace. The faint scent of aftershave lotion filled the room.

"Interesting," she commented, trying to hide the rush of desire that filled her. "What's next?"

Ben left the door open and moved on. "The next room is a guest bedroom."

"Only one? I thought you said there were five."

"The other rooms are empty. I've never bothered to furnish them. Maybe that can be your job.

"Maybe," she answered, on her way to the next room.

"By the way, in case you're wondering, Manuel's quarters are downstairs. They don't count."

Melinda swallowed a smile. If he was trying to tell her they had the privacy to explore their relationship, he had another thing coming.

He opened the door to the room next to his.

Melinda glanced inside the room. There was a smaller four-poster bed. A table and two chairs were set before a large window that overlooked a swimming pool. An orchard, alive with spring blossoms, paraded into the distance. The only other furnishings was a tall dresser. Like the master bedroom, it was decorated in shades of gray. She caught a glimpse of a marble-and-gold bathroom. "Does your room connect to this one?"

"No, but I'm sure it could be arranged." He raised an eyebrow. "Why, are you interested?"

Darn, she'd put her foot in it again! The man had a one-track mind, and it was always on the same track. He'd promised to let her decide when and if their relationship would become more than platonic, but that hadn't stopped him.

"No thank you. You could use a female interior decorator," Melinda added as she surveyed the spartan room. "This room isn't fit for a woman, either."

"There wasn't one in the picture at the time the house was built. That's where you come in," Ben replied airily. "You can have the rooms redecorated any way that pleases you. In fact, everything in

Ritchie Morrison's furniture store is yours to choose from.''

Melinda protested. ''I really can't afford to...''

Ben cut her off brusquely. ''Nonsense. As my wife, you won't have to pay for a thing. ''I take care of my own,'' he added. His lopsided smile and sultry gaze did a number on her.

Without his actually touching her, Melinda felt as if she'd been caressed. Answering shivers of desire swept over her. ''I'm not yours, Ben Howard. Not yet!''

''You will be.'' His gaze brushed her cheeks.

Melinda drew back. ''In name only!''

''Ah! Does that mean you've decided to go along with me?''

''Only as far as the altar—maybe.'' She took a step backward and found herself with her back against the wall. In a bedroom, of all places! ''And, since you're right about us having to live together for a short time, I'll take one of the other bedrooms.''

Pinned against the wall with his hands braced on each side of her head, Melinda had no choice but to look up into his eyes.

''You're sure you don't want to share mine?''

''Ben...'' she warned into the electricity that crackled between them. She could feel its heat. ''You promised!''

''Only until *you* give me the go-ahead.''

''That'll be a cold...'' Her voice broke off when he leaned over and kissed her lips. ''Ben,'' she whispered into his kiss, ''I haven't said yes.''

He took her in his arms and smiled into her eyes.

"Not in so many words, but your eyes are doing the speaking for you. No, don't be embarrassed," he said when she started to protest, "it's no crime to want me as much as I want you."

"That's biology," she murmured. "I told you I wanted more from a relationship than biology. I want a man who cares for me."

"I have a feeling this could turn into a lot more than biology," he replied, stroking her lips. "Since we *are* engaged to be married, why don't we find out just what there is between us?"

He stood so close to her she could feel his body heat. She steeled herself to ignore it. Her response was swift and sure.

Mesmerized by Ben's sensuous voice and the way her body responded to his invitation, she raised her lips to his. She felt his arousal against her body, and his heated gaze shocked her awake. It was time to draw the line before it was too late.

Chapter Six

"Melinda?"

Melinda tore her gaze from the window that looked out over the park. She'd been so deep in thought reliving yesterday afternoon she hadn't heard her aunt come in. Instead, she'd been wondering how she could have walked away from Ben when she wanted so badly to stay.

The answer was clear. She was in love with Ben. Too bad he wasn't in love with her.

"I'm fine, Aunt Bertie. I was just thinking." But she wasn't fine, not really. Physically yes, emotionally no.

She'd thought her experience with her former fiancé had cured her of reading love into a physical relationship no matter how the sparks flew. Perhaps because those sparks hadn't lasted beyond the first few months of their engagement. She'd felt those sparks with Ben yesterday. It had taken all of her determination to ask him to take her home. What good was pride when all she could think of now was what could have been.

"What about, dear? You looked so deep in thought. But then, I suppose all young women are when they're in love and about to get married."

"In love?" Melinda echoed wistfully. Ben's reaction when she'd tried to tell him she couldn't take lovemaking casually had been enough to show her love didn't have to have anything to do with it. Not where men were concerned. His reaction didn't come as a surprise. He was all male, physically and mentally.

Her aunt joined her in glancing out the window. "I've always thought the park was a perfect place to get married. You were so wise to choose it."

"Who was the man you were in love with, Aunt Bertie? Would it hurt you too much to talk about it?"

"No, dear. It was so long ago, I'm afraid it's become a dim memory." Her aunt gazed at a bridal mannequin dressed in an elegant lace confection and sighed. "I was twenty when I met and fell in love with a man I thought was the most handsome and the most wonderful man in the world."

"Here, in Ojai?"

"I was playing the piano at a party when he came up and asked me to play his favorite song." Her aunt's eyes lit up at the memory. "The piece was 'The Blue Danube Waltz.'"

Melinda had always known her aunt was sentimental, but she'd never thought of her as a young woman in love. "And then what happened?"

Dimples appeared in her aunt's cheeks. Her eyes took on a sparkle. "When I finished playing, he took me in his arms and waltzed me around the patio.

There wasn't any real music to dance to, you under-stand. Instead, he hummed the melody in my ear. For the first time in my life, I felt I knew what it meant to be in love.''

''That's the most romantic story I've ever heard,'' Melinda said softly.

''Yes, I suppose it was. Anyway, we spent the whole holiday together. He was home from college on Christmas holiday and due to go to school in two weeks. He took me on long drives along the ocean. South to Santa Barbara to visit the mission and north along the coast highway to Big Sur. Once, we even had a weenie roast on the beach—just the two us. We roasted hot dogs and marshmallows and spent the night looking up at the stars.'' She paused and smiled wistfully. ''I must say, those were the two most ex-citing weeks of my life.''

''And?'' Melinda prodded gently. ''And then?''

''Nothing, I'm afraid. He returned east to school. I waited for a letter, or a postcard, but none came. He was finishing his senior year, and I suppose he was too busy to remember me. I soon began to realize I was a foolish young girl living a dream. I'm afraid the dream ended when I heard he married someone else.''

''Who was he, Aunt Bertie? Did you ever meet him again?''

''It doesn't matter, dear. When we saw each other, it was never the same.''

Taken aback by her aunt's unhappy story, Melinda wanted to strangle the man who had left town without saying goodbye. "Gosh, Aunt Bertie, that's a sad memory to carry around all these years."

"Some of it was wonderful," her aunt protested. "But that's all in the past. I don't think about it very often." The faraway look in her eyes belied her protest.

Melinda put her arms around her aunt and hugged her.

"Is that why you started the bridal shop? To share in other women's weddings?"

"Well, yes," her aunt conceded with a light laugh. "I guess I'm a hopeless romantic. But to tell the truth, I never thought I would stay in business this long. I planned on saving enough money to travel around the world. To places I'd read about and wanted to visit."

"But I came along to keep you here, didn't I?"

"Yes, and I've never regretted it. I've managed very well without seeing the world. And now," she added happily, there's your wedding to Benjamin. I'm truly blessed."

Melinda's heart ached for her aunt, and for herself. One-sided or not, her aunt had had a brief love affair some time in the past. And now it was her turn to care for someone who didn't care for her.

Strange that they had both fallen in love with men who couldn't recognize the real thing when they saw her. "I'm so sorry, Aunt Bertie."

Her aunt returned her hug. "Thank you, dear."

Before her aunt had interrupted her musings, Melinda had felt certain the right thing to do was to release Ben from his agreement. To tell him he didn't have to go through with their make-believe wedding.

She didn't want an "agreement." Not when she still yearned for a real marriage to a man who loved her. And who would give her children.

She'd never dreamed she would settle for a marriage that was little more than a business deal. But the more she learned about her aunt and the sacrifices she'd made for her, the more she realized she was being selfish in turning Ben down.

"And now Benjamin will be part of my family, too," her aunt went on happily as she turned away to right a veil on the mannequin. "And one day, if the good Lord wills, there will be your children to love." She gazed fondly at Melinda. "I must be the luckiest woman in the world."

Melinda watched her aunt move around the showroom for a few moments before wandering off into the kitchen. How could she break her aunt's heart by backing out of the wedding now? If marrying Ben was going to be the answer to keeping the smile on her aunt's face, she had to go through with the fantasy wedding she created.

The doorbell rang. "I'll get it!" Melinda called. She opened the door to Frank, the Valley Florist's delivery boy.

"I have a delivery for a…" He studied the card on the long green florist's box for a moment. "Someone called Tildy."

"I'm sorry, there's no one here by that name." Melinda craned her neck to glance at the card Frank held in his hand. "Are you sure you have the right address?"

"Yep." He held out the card that came with the delivery. "See, take a look for yourself."

"Who's there, dear?" Melinda's aunt came to the door. "Oh, how sweet. Flowers from Benjamin?"

"No," Melinda replied with a wry smile. After the way they'd parted yesterday, the last thing Ben would do would be to send her roses. "Actually, there's been some mistake. The flowers are for someone named Tildy."

Aunt Bertie reached for box. "They're for me, dear."

"For you? The card is addressed to 'Tildy'!"

"Yes, I know." Her aunt opened the box and drew aside the green florist paper. "Of course," she murmured softly. "Yellow roses; for remembrance."

Melinda was transfixed by the look of joy that came over her aunt's face. "Remembrance?" She glanced over her aunt's shoulder at the card, blank except for the name her aunt said was hers. "Who sent them, Aunt Bertie?"

"Someone I knew a long time ago." Her aunt said matter-of-factly, almost as if she'd expected the roses. She gently touched a satin petal. "I'll just go and put them in water," she said with a vague nod at Melinda. "Do give Frank something for his trouble, dear."

Melinda watched as her aunt seemed to float away into the kitchen. She dug into her jeans pocket for a tip. "Thanks, Frank."

"No problem," he said happily as he waved the five-dollar bill Melinda had given him in the air. "Any time!"

Melinda closed the door behind him. She hadn't

glanced at the bill in her pocket. Too bad. It was money they couldn't afford to lose. Still, it had been worth every dollar to see the dreamy expression on her aunt's face. Who was the man who'd sent the roses? And why now, after all those empty years.

She couldn't bring herself to ask again; her aunt was entitled to her own private dreams. Melinda had the premonition that the flower delivery was somehow tied in with the publicity of her own coming wedding to Ben.

TO MELINDA'S DISMAY, after the arrival of the roses, her aunt became more romantic than ever. In spite of Melinda's protestations, plans for her bridal shower had grown more secretive and elaborate every day.

The day of the shower approached. Melinda wore a lime-green sleeveless dress with white accessories. Bertie was dressed in the fashion of the sixties: a full skirted dress, white gloves and hat. Melinda hid a smile. Her aunt seemed to be hopelessly mired in the past. If she still craved adventure, it wasn't showing by the way she dressed.

"Aunt Bertie," Melinda whispered behind a studied smile, as they approached Zoe's Tea Shop. "Are you sure you know what you're doing?"

"I do, dear," her aunt answered happily. "Why don't you go in and enjoy yourself. I'll just wait here by the door for a few minutes in case anyone else shows up."

Melinda kept a fixed smile on her face as she opened the door to the tea room.

"Surprise!"

Melinda blinked as voices hollered in unison. There before her eyes, in Zoe's Tea Shop no less, were a number of her aunt's friends as well as her own. What really blew her mind was the number of uncomfortable male guests trying to make themselves comfortable on the fragile rattan furniture. Men at a bridal shower? Melinda's heart took a dive.

Lace-covered tables were piled high with versions of Zoe's standard high-tea menu: cucumber and watercress sandwiches, scones and biscuits, clobbered cream and strawberry jam. The only difference seemed to be the addition of fortune cookies. And the presence of the uncomfortable male guests.

Melinda stepped backward. "Aunt Bertie," she whispered, "what are those men doing here!"

"It's a couple's shower," her aunt said happily. "Josie Morrison, she's Ritchie Morrison's wife you know, suggested it. It's so much more exciting than an old-fashioned shower, don't you think?"

"Ritchie Morrison, the furniture dealer? What does he have to do with this?"

"Ritchie is Benjamin's best friend. He and Josie helped me plan the shower."

Melinda took a closer look. Ritchie Morrison was dressed in blue jeans, a pale-blue dress shirt, a coat and a tie. Beside him, an equally uncomfortable Ben was dressed in khakis, a beige shirt, coat and a paisley tie. They both looked more accustomed to a bowling alley instead of a tearoom. She swallowed the facetious comment she ached to make.

She didn't like the way Ritchie was eyeing her, either. Did he know the truth about her and Ben's relationship and the platonic marriage they'd agreed on? For sure, the men's presence meant that Ben was as determined as ever to go through with the wedding. Maybe insurance that she wouldn't back out now. "A couples shower in a *tea* shop? Aunt Bertie, it must have cost a fortune!"

"Not at all. Zoe and I have an agreement to barter our respective talents. A verbal barter agreement is just like a contract, dear. As long as Zoe was agreeable to the idea of a couples shower in exchange for her granddaughter's wedding dress, I didn't see any reason not to go through with it. In fact, Ritchie and his wife convinced me you would enjoy it. Let's go on inside. I can hardly wait to see the entertainment they told me they have planned!"

Melinda closed her eyes and said a silent prayer. If the grin on Ritchie's face was a sign, the entertainment was bound to send the hairs on the back of her neck straight up. She glanced at Zoe, Martha Ebbetts and the rest of her aunt's friends. If she guessed right about the entertainment the Morrisons had planned, the hair on the back of their necks would be standing straight up, too. She let her aunt take her by the hand and lead her inside the tearoom to a sea of expectant faces.

In the corner of the room, she saw Ritchie grinning. Ben was trying to make himself scarce. He looked about as uncomfortable as she felt. Good, she thought. She would have hated it if he was having a good time.

"Let's get started with the games," Josie Morrison announced, when, to Melinda's dismay, everyone had read their fortune cookies with sexual innuendos aloud and were still laughing. She passed out sheets of paper and pencils. "Everyone gets to write their advice for the bride and groom on their wedding night." Shouts of renewed laughter filled the small room. Josie held up a warning hand. "Keep the advice clean and romantic because when you're through, I'm going to read them aloud."

Melinda wished she were any place but here in the tearoom. Martha Ebbetts, seated at the side of the room with a small notebook in her hand ready to take notes, tittered at Josie Morrison's remark. The elderly Zoe covered her lips with her hand. Hiding a smile? Bertie and her close friends seemed to be keeping their cool. Melinda said another silent prayer.

"Are you sure you want to go through with this?" Melinda whispered to her aunt. "I have a feeling things might get a little out of hand."

"Of course I am, dear," her aunt answered after a moment's hesitation. "I realize things are a bit different now than when I was a young girl. So much more out in the open. Although—" she peered at Josie, then went on "—I sometimes wonder if some things were better not mentioned in public."

"Amen," Melinda murmured. But she didn't hold out much hope that many of the guests shared the feeling. Bertie was right—society *was* open. If her aunt was ready to accept society as it came, then maybe *she* was the old-fashioned one.

From the way events were headed, Melinda prayed her aunt's open mind would hold up during the rest of the shower.

After a great deal of whispered conversation and

hurried consultations, Josie, in a denim jumper and T-shirt, collected the papers. She shuffled through them and grinned broadly. "What do you know. There must be dozens of ways to be romantic!"

Melinda swallowed a comment. She wasn't exactly a novice in the game of love, but *dozens* of pieces of advice for making love? She reached for a glass of ice water.

"Ready?"

Josie read off the bits of advice in quick succession.

"One. Red roses stand for love. Cover the bed with red rose petals.

"Two. Put a dish of green M&M's on the night-stand. They're a great aphrodisiac.

"Three. *Talk* to her!"

The room broke into laughter. "Talk, on a wedding night?" a male voice asked.

"You bet!" a female voice replied. "Sexual talk is better than M&M's to get you in the mood."

Melinda felt herself blush. The one time she'd tried to talk to Ben about not making love without being in love hadn't seemed to make a difference. They had both been sexually aroused. From what she recalled, their lovemaking wouldn't have needed green M&M's. And, now that she thought of it, talking wouldn't have been necessary, either.

"Four." Josie went on amid more laughter. "Spill a glass of wine on your partner's middle, then slowly lick it up! There are four of you with the same advice," she said into the roar of laughter. "Must work!

"Five. Play romantic music to get in the mood." She raised her voice over more sensual comments.

"Six. Put a romantic note under her pillow for her to find in the morning."

Melinda tuned out the rest of the bits of erotic advice and tried to concentrate on why she was here in the first place: to save Bertie from the embarrassment of bankruptcy. Somehow, even that excuse didn't ring true.

She was honest enough to admit she was here because she was tempted to marry the man of her dreams. Even if it was going to be in a fake ceremony. And even though he didn't love her.

If she hadn't been tempted, why was she concentrating on some of the more erotic pieces of advice Josie was avidly reading aloud?

"Kiss every freckle he or she has on his or her body." "Rub peach brandy across each other's bodies and lick it up...very slowly."

From the dark look Ben was giving his friend Ritchie, Melinda had a good idea who had come up with that idea. It hadn't been in a fortune cookie.

"Take a shower together with scented soap and body lotion."

"Maybe we'd better open the gifts now," Josie finally announced above the laughter. She glanced through the remaining slips of papers. "The rest of the suggestions aren't fit for mixed company."

Melinda drained her glass of ice water.

"Good idea," Josie's husband loudly agreed. "Open the gifts. I can't wait to see the Victoria's Secret lingerie and nightgowns!"

"Ritchie Morrison, watch it!" his wife cautioned with a deadly look. "There are ladies present! And you, Ben Howard, come on up here and help your bride open your presents.''

Ben ambled up to the head table and smiled back affably at the guests. There was steel in his voice and amusement in his eyes as he fixed Ritchie with a studied smile. ''Anyone who gets out of line answers to me.''

''In that case,'' Ritchie shouted, ''you'd better forget about the lingerie.''

''No way,'' Ben said with a sidelong glance at Melinda. ''After all I've heard and seen about Victoria's Secret, I'm kind of looking forward to seeing them for myself. Just don't ask my bride to model.''

His bride! Melinda swallowed a retort. Ben and his one-track mind! If he was playing for public consumption, he had the audience in the palm of his hand. Her, too. But, she suspected that the last way he thought of her was as his true bride.

She opened the first gift and held up a cup and saucer to a matching set of dishes. Thank goodness, there was no sexual connotation here. ''Service for eight!''

Ben took his turn. To her relief, the gift, when unwrapped, turned out to be a mundane car vacuum!

Melinda began to relax. So far, so good.

Ben handed her the next gift with a grin that told her he sensed her apprehension of the contents. The box contained a year's supply of green M&M's wrapped in passionate red cellophane.

Before Ben could comment on the color of the candy-covered chocolates, Melinda turned a fixed smile on him. ''Your turn next, *dear.*''

She regretted handing him the box as soon as he opened it and pulled out a flimsy robe and matching negligee. "These must be for you, *honey*. They're definitely not my style."

Melinda ignored the teasing exchange of lover's endearments. If Ben was trying to save face for her, he was overdoing it. She reached for the next gift.

A set of gourmet pots and pans. "I hope you can cook, *sweetheart*," Ben announced. "I can scramble eggs, but that's as far as I can go."

She'd already told him she couldn't cook, but she went along with the charade. Anything to keep him in line so he wouldn't embarrass her with sexual innuendos. "As long as you don't expect anything fancy, you needn't worry."

Melinda opened the next gift of two boxes tied together that turned out to be a matching set of his and hers bathrobes. Her look dared him to comment.

She watched while Ben took another turn and came up with a cocktail shaker and six crystal goblets. "The gifts are going back as soon as decently possible," she murmured. "We can't possible keep them."

"We can't?"

"No," she answered with a studied smile. "We agreed that ours was going to be temporary relationship, remember?" She tried to hide the unhappiness in her voice as she thought of slick bodies tumbling together on the massive guest-room bed at Ben's house—provided she would have been willing.

Ben looked noncommittal, but she could guess what he was thinking.

Ignoring Ben's presence at Melinda's side, Martha Ebbetts moved her chair closer to Melinda. "So tell us, dear," she asked when the vanilla ice cream and Bertie's chocolate-chip cookies were being served. "How *did* you manage to get Ben to propose? He's been our favorite bachelor for so long, the rest of us gave up on him."

A sudden silence fell on the room.

Ignoring the interested look on Ben's face as he waited for her answer, Melinda borrowed her aunt's favorite expression. "I guess it was fate, Ms. Ebbetts." She poked Ben in the ribs when he opened his mouth. "Wasn't it, dear?"

"You bet, sweetheart!" he agreed with a cough of pain. "Although I'd have to say the connection was more like love at first sight."

A hush fell over the room at Melinda's answer and Ben's romantic contribution. Josie looked reproachfully across the room at her husband. Ritchie smiled sheepishly.

"Fate! What a lovely way to explain love at first sight," Martha Ebbetts cooed. She beamed at Melinda and Ben. "I must use that as the headline of my report for tomorrow's newspaper. And don't worry. I'll make sure you have an extra copy of the paper for your bridal memory book."

"Do be sure to include your answers in your wedding vows," Bertie said happily. She dug a watered taffeta and lace photo album out of the stack of gifts. "You can use this to file away the newspaper story. It will be a nice way to start the album. I'm sure you'll want your children to share your romantic memories with you.''

Wedding vows! Bridal memory books! Children! Melinda swayed at the thought of exchanging empty marriage vows with Ben. And at the mention of the children she might never have. It was only the pressure of the arm Ben quickly threw around her shoulders that kept her upright in her chair.

On the pretext of kissing her, he leaned over and kissed the tip of her ear. ''Are you okay? I can spring us out of here anytime you're ready.''

Melinda returned the kiss with a sigh and leaned into his arms. He smelled of vanilla ice cream and her aunt's cookies, more of an aphrodisiac than M&M's ever would be.

Conscious of everyone's avid eyes on her, Melinda shook her head. ''I just got dizzy for a minute.'' If ever there was a point of no return, she thought as she looked up into Ben's concerned gaze as he bent to kiss her again, this was surely it.

After the public display of their supposed romantic relationship, she simply had no choice. She had to go through with the wedding.

And what would come after that, heaven only knew.

Chapter Seven

"Hey, Ben! You in there?" A heavy fist pounded on Ben's office door.

Ben's head snapped up at the unwelcome sound of Ritchie's voice. After his coed bridal shower idea, Ritchie was the last person he wanted to see. Wasn't there any place a man could do some serious thinking? He considered the chance that Ritchie would go away if he asked him to.

"Ben?" The pounding resumed.

"Just a minute." Ben dropped his pen, unlocked the office door and surveyed his good-humored friend. "Come on in, if you have to."

Ritchie inched his way into Ben's office. "I called at the house first. When there was no answer, I came over here." He studied Ben. "You don't sound glad to see me."

Ben shrugged. "I was thinking."

Ritchie glanced at his wristwatch and surveyed the dimly lit office. "In the dark?"

"Yeah, well, I had a lot to think about."

"At eight o'clock on a Saturday night? Without Melinda?"

"I had something important to think about." Ben turned over the pad of paper he'd been doodling on so Ritchie couldn't see he'd been writing her name over and over again. He couldn't get her out of his mind. Only, instead of writing Melinda Carey, he'd found himself writing Melinda Howard.

"Sounds serious. Need some help?"

Ben decided to accept the inevitable. "If you won't go away, you might as well sit down." Ritchie sat. "The truth is, I was thinking of Melinda and her strange reaction at the bridal shower. I thought she was going to faint."

"She sick?"

"I don't think so. She looked perfectly healthy before the shower."

"Josie thinks Melinda was having bridal jitters. She says all brides get nervous before the wedding," Ritchie added with a grin.

"And here I thought it was only the groom who felt that way." Ben wasn't about to tell Ritchie that Melinda had looked great the other day when he'd invited her to see his home.

On the pretext they could go over plans to decorate a bedroom for her use after they were married, he'd invited her to spend the night. She'd agreed to redecorate a room and, for a few breathtaking moments, he'd actually thought she'd agree to stay. He'd wound up taking her home, but he'd taken her choosing a room as a good omen for the future—for all of twenty-four hours. Then came the shower when she'd almost fainted in his arms.

A couple's shower? He relived the moment in his mind. No wonder Melinda had been upset. For a while he'd thought she was enjoying herself. Until something or someone had said something to upset her. Was it something he had said?

Damn Ritchie and his crazy ideas!

Ritchie slid into a chair, leaned back and inhaled the sweet scent of aging fruit brandy that permeated the small office. "God, I sure love this place. My own office smells of pine furniture, carpeting and furniture polish." He took another deep breath.

"Women," Ritchie went on to say knowingly, "you never know what they're up to from one moment to the next." He paused. His face lit up. "Say, you're not expecting, are you?"

Ben rolled his eyes.

"Sorry," Ritchie grinned. "I didn't mean anything. You guys *are* engaged. But whatever was wrong with Melinda, I gotta tell you she sure looked beautiful. Heck, if I weren't a happily married man, I'd be thinking about her, too."

Ritchie's grin faded at Ben's frown. "Sorry, I guess I got carried away. Anything else is on your mind?"

"A couple of things. How good are you on the Internet, Ritch?"

His friend blinked at the abrupt change in subject. "As in computer?"

"Yeah, as in computer Web sites."

Ritchie grin reappeared. "I wasn't going to mention it, but I did hear your photograph is on an Internet dating service. Funny, seeing as how you and Melinda are going to get married. For that matter,'' he added admiringly, ''half of the single women in Ojai would have been happy to date you. And some of the married ones, too.''

Ben swallowed a sharp retort. In spite of his friend's protests, he still had a suspicion the guy was behind putting Ben's photograph on the Web site. He might deny it, but if it turned out to be true, Ritchie's days were numbered. ''You put my photograph on there?''

''No way!'' Ritchie protested. ''You're barking up the wrong tree. I don't know a damn thing about computers, thank God. I'm perfectly happy running my furniture store and coaching Little League baseball in my spare time. I leave fooling around with computers to my bookkeeper. Why?''

Ben wasn't convinced. There was something behind the laughter in Ritchie's eyes that told him he had *something* to do with it. He might think the Web site caper was funny, but *he* didn't. ''Just a thought.''

''Seems to me you've been inhaling brandy fumes too long, buddy. There's more to your question than meets the eye. What's up?''

Ben gazed at the man who had been his closest friend for ten years. He had to talk to someone or go crazy. Common sense may have deserted him but his thoughts were in a turmoil. He had to talk to someone.

He strode to a large wall cabinet. He considered the array of exotic bottles filled with fruit brandies brewed by his distillery before he chose an apricot brandy. "I think we can both use some of this."

"Any time," Ritchie said happily. "Something tells me this is going to be more serious than I thought."

Ben gathered two small brandy snifters from the shelf and stepped back to the desk. "Here, you pour while I talk."

Between sips of brandy, Ben told Ritchie how he'd discovered he was about to become a married man. He left out the more intimate details of the platonic marriage and the promise he'd made to Melinda. He couldn't complain. He was going through with the wedding ceremony as much for his own sake as hers.

"The whole wedding thing started as a mistake," he began when Ritchie's laughter stopped him.

"Hell!" Ritchie almost choked on his laughter. "And here I thought it was a case of love at first sight."

"I wish. The truth is, Melinda and I were in high school together, maybe even danced at Friday night socials a time or two. But the truth is I don't actually remember her."

"How could you forget someone like Melinda for God's sakes?"

"You're right." Ben agreed with a wry smile. "Especially if she looked anything like she does today. The truth is Melinda actually chose me as a bridegroom off that damn dating Web site you both say you have nothing to do with. She said she was fooling around with a make-believe marriage intended for her own amusement. And that what happened next was an innocent mistake.''

Ritchie moved to the edge of his chair. ''An amusement?'' Is that what she calls a wedding? Heck, this is better than the soaps,'' he said cheerfully. ''I can't wait until I tell Josie about it!''

Ben glowered. ''Over your dead body!''

Ritchie threw up his arms in surrender. ''Okay, okay, so what happens next?''

Ben shrugged. He stared into the sweet smelling liqueur that remained on the bottom of the snifter. ''We're getting married.''

''Married to Melinda Carey by mistake! How lucky can a guy get?'' Ritchie sat back and beamed his admiration.

Ben eyed Ritchie. ''And the photograph on the Internet? Did you put it there?''

''I told you you've got the wrong guy! I wouldn't do that, at least not to you!''

''Yeah, sure,'' Ben muttered. Under any other circumstances, the earnest expression on Ritchie's face would have been comical. As it was, he didn't believe him for a moment. ''And I'm not going to apologize until I find the jackass who did.''

''So, now what?''

''I told you. I'm going to get married next Saturday. In a public park, no less.'' Ben drained his brandy snifter. ''By the way, did I forget to ask you to be my best man?''

''No problem.'' Ritchie hesitated. ''But to be honest, no one in his right mind would expect you to go through with the wedding. Not under the circumstances you described.''

''That's the real problem,'' Ben conceded. He drained his brandy snifter. ''I don't think I *am* in my right mind. And, from the looks of things, neither is Melinda. And that's only part of the story.'' He went on to tell Ritchie about his uncle's ultimatum.

Ritchie reached for a refill and slumped in his chair. ''What a mess!''

A mess? Hardly. Ben thought of the near-picnic at the distillery. Of Melinda's searching green eyes, the taste of her soft lips and the way his body had stirred before she'd delivered the bad news that she couldn't make love with a man who didn't love her. Or at least care for her. At the time, he hadn't had the answer she'd been looking for.

She'd said their mutual attraction was pure biology, of all the stupid things! Biology be damned! After ten years of sampling pure biology, he was beginning to think the attraction he felt for her was something more complicated.

Caring? Yes. Love? Not yet. But that hadn't stopped him from wanting her so badly that he'd ached for hours.

The trouble was, he'd been down that road before. He'd vowed that the next time he decided he loved someone, he was going to be damn sure both he and the woman involved meant it.

He reflected on his brief, early marriage. After ten years, he still couldn't explain that brief period when he'd thought he'd found the right woman. Three months later, they'd said goodbye. He hadn't met anyone who fit the bill since. Not until Melinda.

"It won't be a sacrifice, Ritch," he said thoughtfully. Not when he considered how passionate Melinda could become under the right circumstances. He might have to wait to share that passion with her, but that was okay, too. Once they went through with the wedding ceremony, there would be plenty of time to convince her they belonged together. "Besides, who knows how it will all turn out in the end?"

Ritchie snorted. "Don't tell me you've talked yourself into falling in love with Melinda!"

"And what if I have?"

"Let's be reasonable. From what you say, you hardly know her, so how could you have fallen in love with her? What happened to the guy who sampled marriage and said he found it wanting?"

Ben shook himself out of his reverie. "Maybe it was the woman I was naive enough to marry, Ritch. Or maybe, we were both too young. On the other hand, not all women are alike. Look at you and Josie. The two of you have been happily married for several years, and you both still look happy."

"Yeah," Ritchie agreed. "Did I tell you Josie's decided we're planning to start a family?"

"No, but congratulations. Here." Ben poured another measure of apricot brandy. "I'll drink to that and a dozen more."

"Not me." Ritchie shuddered. "I'll take them one at a time. Now, back to your wedding next Saturday. I'm happy to be your best man, but are you sure you still want to get married?"

"Damn sure!" Ben drained his snifter.

"If you say so," Ritchie answered, draining his own. "It's your life. Which reminds me of why I'm here. I came to take you to an impromptu bachelor party."

"A bachelor party?" Ben's thoughts swung back to the couples shower and Melinda's reaction. "Not another coed party, for God's sakes!" He couldn't keep a note of horror out of his voice.

"Hell no! I'm talking about a *bachelor's* party." Ritchie shuddered. "Come on, let's go."

Ben hesitated. "Wait a minute! Where is this party?"

"Not at the tea shop," Ritchie laughed. "It's at the bowling alley. So, just forget your problems for tonight and prepare to enjoy the fun. Look at it this way—this is your chance to kiss your bachelor days goodbye."

Ben regarded his best friend quizzically. "Okay, but no surprises! I have to be in shape for the wedding."

Ritchie froze. "Any doubts that you *are* in shape?"

"Not that I know of," Ben muttered. "It's just that it's been a while since I took the time to find out." *Not that it really mattered,* he added to himself. It looked as if he wasn't going to be called upon to put his manhood to the test any time soon. Just the thought of sleeping with Melinda sent heat coursing through him. He got to his feet and wiped his hand across his forehead. "It's either gotten too warm in here or I'm plain tired."

"It's the brandy, my man," Ritchie said with an

appreciative glance around the office. "What a way to go! But buck up, the night is young and the best is yet to come."

"Nothing obscene, I hope," Ben cautioned, knowing full well he couldn't take the chance of putting himself in harm's way. "I'm not in the mood."

"Saving yourself for Melinda?"

Ben grimaced. If his friend only knew the truth. He was ready, willing and able. It was Melinda and her old-fashioned ideas that were the problem. "Okay, okay. Let's go."

Cheers and sexual innuendos sounded when Ben walked into the private room at the back of the bowling alley. He grit his teeth and smiled. It didn't take long for him to find out he was the last person his friends were interested in. The fun had already started and their collective minds were focused on someone more interesting.

Eastern music wailed its minor beat. To an occasional loud whoop or a shout of encouragement, a busty belly dancer slowly wove her way around the room. She was dressed—if you could call it being dressed, Ben thought wryly—in layered colored scarves and a sheer, beaded skirt that displayed her substantial charms. Dollar bills were stuck in her cleavage and around the banded skirt that hung low around her hips.

She had rings on her fingers and bells on her toes. Long, silver strands of tiny tinkling bells dangled from her ears. She pouted under a sheer veil and clanged tiny cymbals between her fingers as she swirled around the room. A diamond stud sparkled at one nostril.

When she sidled up to him, he was shocked to find her sheer skirt covered an almost-nude body. He held his breath when she bowed and the skirt looked ready to slide off her ample hips. The effect mesmerized him and awed the guests.

"Welcome, master," she whispered.

Ben looked around the room. "You've got the wrong guy."

She smiled and slowly glided around him, her arms drawing him in. He shook his head. She glided on.

The dancer looked ripe and ready, but after his initial reaction, Ben tried not to be interested. Instead, he concentrated on the cotton dress that had covered Melinda at their aborted picnic.

Maybe more was better for a man's libido if he was going to be called upon to put it to a test.

When it became obvious no one was paying attention to him, the guest of honor, Ben realized he might as well have stayed at home.

"Where did you find the star of the evening on such short notice?" he asked Ritchie, his wary glance on the dancer's come-hither movements. "She can't live in Ojai, or the guys wouldn't be ogling her as if they've never seen her before."

"That's Angie, Josie's cousin down from San Francisco," Ritchie remarked, his attention on the exotic dancer. He handed Ben a cold beer. "Drink up and enjoy. Angie says she dances to keep in shape. Not bad, eh?"

No, Ben thought as he watched the dancer undulate

her way back to his side, the lady wasn't bad at all. She had sex appeal to spare, and looked ready to prove it. He was surprised to find he wasn't all that interested.

And then it hit him. Josie Morrison was a blue-eyed blonde with Sweden written all over her. The dancer, on the other hand, had midnight-black hair and deep-brown eyes outlined with kohl. Her eyelashes were darkened with mascara, her eyelids colored with green eye shadow. And skin that spoke of hot Mediterranean nights and Italian love songs.

If Angie was Josie's cousin, he was a monkey's uncle.

All the more reason to believe Ritchie was the clown behind the dating Web site that had started the scenario that was turning him into a married man.

The music grew frenzied. The dancer swayed provocatively from side to side and shook her cleavage under his nose. Ben almost choked on his beer. How could a woman's body go in three directions at one time?

To his discomfiture, the dancer languidly handed him one of the scarves that covered her ample breasts and gave him a seductive smile.

He swallowed hard.

The dancer turned her back and motioned an invitation for him to untie another scarf that covered a strategic area. He clutched the ice-cold beer in the vain hope it would cool the fire the dancer ignited in him.

"No thanks," he said politely, but firmly, more to himself than the dancer, "I think I'll sit this one out."

She pouted and slithered over to Ritchie. With a choked apology and a reluctant grin at Ben, he tucked a ten-dollar bill in the scarf that covered her breasts, patted her on her shoulder and sent her on her way. "Sorry, sweetheart. I'm sitting this one out, too."

"Ritch," Ben began when they were alone again, "you said this was going to be a harmless diversion with no surprises. You have no idea what this is doing to me!"

"I don't remember the harmless," Ritchie laughed, "but what the hell. What could surprises hurt? You're single until next Saturday."

When Ben discovered he wasn't as immune to the exotic dancer as he thought, he downed the beer and headed for a table loaded with chips and pretzels and green M&M's. Looking back at the action over his shoulder, Ritchie reluctantly trailed after him. "What's next? A stripper?"

"Yeah! The guys wanted to go the whole nine yards."

Ben was afraid to ask for a definition of "whole nine yards." He only knew he had to get out of here before he compromised himself. "A belly dancer *and* a stripper? Don't tell me she's Josie's cousin, too?"

Ritchie tried to look innocent, but in Ben's mind it didn't compute. Guilt was written all over the guy.

Ben studied the grin on his friend's face. It was all too easy. Was Ritchie behind the Web site after all? "How did you know I was going to wind up getting married? You had this all planned well in advance, didn't you?"

"The wedding announcement in the newspaper,

that's how,'' Ritchie answered. ''After seeing that, hell, I decided you deserved the best.'' He couldn't seem to look into Ben's eyes.

Ben kept his thoughts to himself, but things were beginning to add up. Ritchie may have denied putting Ben's picture on the dating Web site, but something about the look in his eyes told him Ritchie had *something* to do with it. A joke was a joke, but the dating Web site caper was carrying things too far.

Ben downed his beer and debated the likelihood of getting Ritchie to admit he was guilty of starting the chain of events that had led Ben to the altar. Fat chance!

Ritchie threw his arm around his shoulders and pulled him into the center of the room. ''Drink up! Wait until you see what's coming next!''

Ben reconciled himself to being a good sport, but he was afraid he'd had enough sexual stimulation to keep him awake all night. No matter what Ritchie came up with next, no way did he intend to satisfy it here.

A drum sounded behind a closed door. A hush fell. To the steady, sensuous beat of the drum, a woman with long red hair streaming down her back wove her way into the room. She was dressed in leopard skins, metal jewelry and a calculating smile.

The tension in the room, already near its peak, rose. The stripper paraded around the room to the sensuous sound of the drum. Ben blinked. Another woman with loose joints! Only this body went north, south, east *and* west at the same time!

The stripper's glance raked Ben in an open invitation. A feral smile covered her lips. She removed pieces of jewelry from her arms and tossed them, one by one at his feet for him to pick up. He couldn't move.

The stripper's clothing followed, piece by piece, until she was clothed in little more than her flowing hair and a feathered G-string. She paraded slowly around Ben, twisting upraised hands and swinging her hips side to side to the slow, steady beat of the recorded drum music.

When their turns came, men rushed to put bills in a fake leopard-skin pouch hung around her neck. At least he hoped it was fake. On the other hand, what leopard wouldn't have been happy to give its life to wrap itself around the stripper's lush body?

To be a good sport, Ben grimly stuck a twenty-dollar bill into her G-string. He was going to be broke before the night was through if this kept up.

He swallowed hard and desperately tried to cling to Melinda's wholesome image. As for Ritchie, if the self-confessed happily married guy had arranged the two performances for Ben's benefit, Ben wasn't buying.

He tried to catch Ritchie's attention to tell him he wanted to leave, but it would have been like taking a kid out of a candy store. When the stripper turned away to find another sucker, Ben spun on his heel and out the door to find a taxi. No one inside was going to miss him.

TO MELINDA'S dismay, her aunt Bertie's romantic dreams turned out to be more grandiose than even

Melinda would have believed possible.

A large white envelope, with Congratulations, You're A Winner written across it, arrived in the mail two days later.

She'd seen this type of envelope before. The crucial word left out was "if...."

Melinda's first instinct was to toss the letter into the wastepaper basket along with all the other misleading prizewinning letters she and the rest of the literate world regularly received. Considering the way her luck was going lately, her second thought was involuntary. Maybe she'd won something, after all. She opened the letter to find a picture of an old-fashioned wedding and an offer someone thought she couldn't refuse.

> "Dear Bride-to-be:
> Congratulations! Your name has been drawn as a first-place winner in a joint promotion between the Happy-Ever-After Bridal Attire Co. and the Pacific Coastal Railroad.
> Accordingly, you have been awarded two tickets for the inaugural departure of the Love Train Honeymoon Tours departing July 9th, from Santa Barbara, California, and continuing to Seattle, Washington.
> Please advise your acceptance by calling 1-800-323-9999."

Melinda froze. How in heaven's name could she have won a honeymoon when she hadn't entered any contest?

She took a deep breath and reread the letter. The letters danced in front of her eyes.

A double suite!

Breakfast in bed!

Champagne!

En suite music!

Optional: a guided tour through Victoria, B.C.

She searched her memory as she stared at the rows of bridal dresses surrounding her and the bridal dress that was waiting for her upstairs in her bedroom. All of them, without an exception, had come from the Happy-Ever-After Bridal Attire Company!

Bertie at work again!

She should have realized her aunt had wider horizons than bridal showers.

She read the letter again. As a longtime client of their business, the Happy-Ever-After Bridal Attire Company must have only been too happy to grant their loyal client's request. As to what her aunt must have bartered or promised to purchase for the favor, Melinda was too stunned to even think about it.

Chapter Eight

It took Ben twenty minutes to show up after Melinda called and asked him to come over. He cursed when she hung up before he had a chance to ask what was wrong. Was she ill? Had she changed her mind again? His heart in his throat, he was sure he'd broken at least a dozen traffic laws before he pulled up in front of Bertie's Bridal Shop and strode inside without knocking.

"Where's the fire? What's up?" His questions came rapidly. "Are you okay?" It wasn't until she waved a paper in front of him that he calmed down.

When Melinda showed him the award letter, one quick look was more than enough to set him off. A honeymoon with a bride he'd promised not to touch until she was ready? It was too much to expect of him. He blew his stack.

"Jeez! I don't believe this!" After his unrequited sexual response at his bachelor party the other night, the idea of a platonic honeymoon was more than he could take.

"Believe it. I called the 800 number and it's not a

fake. But please keep your voice down,'' she muttered. "I don't want to upset my aunt.''

"Upset your aunt?'' He studied the letter again. "What does she have to do with this?''

"You wouldn't believe me if I told you.''

Ben grit his teeth. "Damn it!'' he muttered after a cautious glance around him. "Since this concerns the both of us, maybe you'd better give me the whole story.'' He paused. "Say, you don't intend to accept the prize do you?''

"No! What do you take me for?'' He shrugged. She glared at him. "As for the letter, it *is* the whole story, at least I hope so. What I'm afraid of is what Aunt Bertie put up to make sure I won the prize.''

Ben's business mind sprang to attention. He gazed around the old but proud surroundings; sparkling glass counters filled with bridal adornments, oak furniture and floors gleaming with years of polish. A small museumlike display of miniature mannequins dressed in a series of bridal gowns dating into the last century filled a glassed-in bookcase. The room and the one across the hall were filled with bridal dresses and had everything a bride could want—except prospective brides. If Bertie was making money with the bridal shop, she kept it well hidden.

He rubbed his brow. When Melinda had called him, she sounded as if she was in deep trouble. From the look of things, maybe she was in deeper than met the eye. "What do you mean, 'put up'? I thought you said your aunt was almost broke!''

"She is. But I'm afraid she may have ordered more bridal gowns and accessories in order to win the prize." Melinda's voice trailed off. She glanced at the door and shrugged helplessly. "Once my aunt gets an idea, there's no stopping her." She dropped to her knees in front of a bridal mannequin.

"Here hold the pin cushion while I finish hemming this wedding gown."

"You think she's going to buy *more* wedding gowns?" His voice rose with his growing frustration. "The whole idea is ridiculous. I thought you said she had no one to sell gowns to!" He waved the letter in the air. "It's beginning to sound as if the wedding arrangements have snowballed out of control!"

"Shhh!" Melinda looked beside herself with anxiety. "Not so loud. Aunt Bertie's not exactly selling the gowns. She probably intends to barter them for services."

"Barter? Barter for what? I thought that practice went out with the pilgrims!"

"That's what I used to think," she agreed. "But that's how she paid for my shower!"

Ben began to believe he was in the vortex of some bad dream. "No problem," he said when he had his voice level and under control. "If we have to return the shower gifts, we can damn well return the prize, too. Now, before it's too late!"

"Ouch!" Melinda stopped to pull a pin out of her finger and looked around for a tissue. "If I get any bloodstains on the gown now..."

"Hang on." Ben raised Melinda to her feet, took her finger and held it to his lips. The look of surprise on Melinda's face was nothing compared to the surprise he felt himself at finding them face-to-face, eye-to-eye, lip-to-lip.

He felt like a fool, but he didn't want the bleeding to stop any time soon. And from the way Melinda was looking at him, he had the idea she wasn't in a rush, either. When she didn't pull away, he sucked on her finger. "This should stop the bleeding," he finally said. What it didn't stop was the way his testosterone was acting up. When he looked up at her, her eyes were glazed. He was sure his were, too. Too bad they were standing in plain sight of anyone who might come into the shop.

"I don't know why your aunt should pay for the wedding anyway." He wrapped his clean handkerchief around her finger and gave it a final squeeze before he let go of her hand. "We're both adults. We can pay for our own wedding." He searched in his pocket for his checkbook. "Just tell me how much you need and I'll write you a check."

Melinda bit her lower lip. The glaze in her eyes disappeared in a flash. "No thanks. If you insist on providing the liquor, that will be enough."

Ben prayed for help to the saints who watched over foolish bridegrooms. "Er, now that you mention it, I have something to tell you."

"Make it something good," she said with a catch in her voice. "I don't know how much more bad news I can take."

He ached to take her back in his arms and kiss that catch away. To tell her he was there for her. That he would always try to make things right for her. Maybe he would chance it—once he gave her the bad news.

"When I applied for the permit to hold the wedding in the park, I'm afraid the fine print outlawed any liquor. So, unless you're planning on holding a wedding reception elsewhere, that shouldn't be a problem. I can scare up lemonade or a fruit punch."

"Don't let my aunt hear you, for heaven's sake!" Melinda whispered frantically. "If she does, she's sure to find another place to hold the reception."

"Not Miss Zoe's Tea Shop for Pete's sake?"

"Heavens no!" Melinda giggled. "Aunt Bertie told me poor Zoe hasn't gotten over the shock of some of the more earthy wedding night suggestions your friends came up with at the shower."

Ben grinned sheepishly. The bridal shower had been a kid's birthday party compared to his bachelor's party. Ritchie was home nursing a doozy of a hangover this minute. Josie wasn't too happy, either. "I don't know about that. She looked mighty interested in what was going on."

"You think so?"

"I think so. But back to the honeymoon award letter. I have to tell you I don't know if a rail honeymoon is a smart idea. To put it bluntly," he said brushing her cheek with his knuckles, "it would be too damn tempting!"

How could he agree to a honeymoon when he couldn't keep his hands off the bride?

He watched Melinda blush. If she was thinking of their near miss at his place last week, so was he.

Now that things began to add up, he remembered her reaction to the mention of their children at their shower. Maybe her panic had come when she'd realized that if she intended to have children, it took two to make a baby. And that he was the only candidate around. He was beginning to like the idea.

"I'll just have to try to get my aunt to cancel the award," Melinda finally announced. "I've been thinking, anyway. I've decided ours should remain a marriage of convenience after all. That's what we initially agreed to, wasn't it?"

Ben shrugged helplessly. He remembered his stupid agreement to wait until Melinda was ready to make love with him. Considering the way he was beginning to feel about her, how could he forget?

MELINDA SURFACED to the sound of her bedroom shutters being thrown open.

"Good morning, dear. It's a lovely day for a wedding!"

Blinded by the bright sunshine that streamed into the room, Melinda cast a bleary eye at the digital clock on the nightstand. Reassured, she murmured a vague reply and burrowed deeper under the blanket.

"Come, dear," her aunt chided. "This is your wedding day." She slid up the casement window and took a deep breath of the scented air that blew into the bedroom. "Lovely," she added, "just lovely."

"It's only eight-thirty," Melinda grumbled, half-awake. She'd spent the night thinking of Ben and marveling that she could still be attracted to him after all that had happened the last few weeks. "What's so lovely at this time of the morning?"

"The gardenia bushes across the street are in full

bloom." Her aunt took another deep breath. "Can't you smell them?"

"Gosh!" Melinda sat up in bed, inhaled and suddenly thought of allergic bridegrooms. "I forgot I ordered the bushes! What if Ben's allergic to gardenias?"

"Don't worry, dear. As long as the wedding is outside, I'm sure there won't be a problem." Her aunt gestured to the tray on the nightstand. "I brought you a cup of coffee to help your day get started."

Melinda reached for the welcome coffee. "Thanks, Aunt Bertie. You always know what I need." She sipped her drink and gazed fondly at her aunt. "How are you doing this morning?"

"I'm fine. Busy, but fine." Her aunt paused in front of the dresser mirror and patted a wisp of her streaked hair into place. "Since I'm going to be in the wedding party, Zoe has graciously agreed to take care of all the last-minute details."

With Zoe even more romantically inclined than her aunt, Melinda shuddered to think of what details Zoe was busy taking care of. Dollar signs floated in front of her eyes.

She swallowed a facetious comment. "The ceremony isn't scheduled until noon. We have plenty of time. Besides, there aren't any last-minute details. I took care of everything when I planned the wedding. That's how I got into this mess in the first place."

"Oh dear. You really shouldn't call your wedding day a mess," her aunt reproved and set about tidying up the room. "You're just having a case of bridal nerves." She paused to gaze reproachfully at Melinda. "I must say, you and Benjamin are one of the most nervous couples I've seen."

Melinda took another uneasy sniff at the strong scent of a dozen gardenia bushes in full bloom that wafted into the room. "You can say that again." She headed for the bathroom. "I'm going to take a long, hot bath and soak myself numb. See you later."

"Oh dear. You *are* in a state, aren't you? I hope that by the time you're bathed and dressed, you'll feel a great deal more like yourself."

"The real me disappeared four weeks ago after I fooled around with the computer," Melinda muttered. Guilty, she paused in her tracks. "I swear, the last thing I expected was to wind up actually getting married to Ben."

"It was your destiny," her aunt said complacently, obviously now back to her dream world. "I'm sure the two of you are going to be very happy."

"Maybe," Melinda answered under her breath, "but I don't have high hopes." How could she be happy with a make-believe marriage, a husband who didn't love her and no chance in the near future for the patter of the little feet she'd dreamed of? No wonder she'd almost fainted at her bridal shower. Dreams died hard.

"Well, if you're sure you don't need me, I think I'll just go along and get myself ready." Her aunt paused at the door and gazed back shyly at Melinda. "I've outfitted many a bridal party, but this the first time I've been in one. Imagine! A maid of honor at my age! You *do* still want me to be your attendant?"

"Of course I do!" Melinda glanced at the clock

and gave up the idea of a long, hot bath. She had a dress to iron and her aunt to keep happy. In a few short hours she'd be playing the role of Mrs. Ben Howard. But first, she had to psyche herself into the right frame of mind or she'd never get through the afternoon.

Her aunt smiled. "I was afraid I was too old to be an attendant. Are you sure?"

Melinda detoured on her way to the bathroom door and hurried to hug her aunt. "Yes, I'm sure, Aunt Bertie. The maid of honor is usually the bride's best friend, and that's exactly what you are to me. Not only my best friend, but the mother I never really knew," she added softly. "You're going to be the most beautiful woman at the wedding. Everyone's eyes will be on you."

"Good heavens, I hope not!" her aunt fluttered. "They're supposed to be looking at the bride!"

"Not this time. When they see you in that beautiful dress with pink roses in your hair, Aunt Bertie, you'll be the hit of the wedding."

"It *is* a pretty dress, isn't it?" her aunt said wistfully. "I've loved it from the moment I ordered it from the catalog. But I never thought *I'd* be the one to wear it."

Melinda impulsively went to her jewelry box and took out a necklace of blush-colored pearls. "Here, wear this with your dress, Aunt Bertie."

"Oh, I couldn't possibly. They were your mother's. Our parents gave it to her on her wedding day."

"Mom was your sister, Aunt Bertie. How come no one ever gave you a pearl necklace?"

"I suppose it's because a pearl necklace is a traditional gift to a bride from her parents to bring the bride good luck. Since I never married, I was never given one." She glanced regretfully at Melinda. "I only wish your mother was here to see you as a bride."

"So do I, Aunt Bertie. But *you're* here!" From the unhappy look that came over her aunt's face, Melinda was sorry she'd brought up the subject of the necklace in the first place.

"Don't be sorry, dear. I've already told you there's nothing to be sorry about. I have my memories."

Melinda's heart ached for her aunt. Her aunt deserved more out of life than memories. Who was the man she'd fallen in love with all those years ago? More to the point, Melinda thought as she threw a light cotton robe around herself, had there been a message in the yellow roses he'd sent her aunt last week? Would the man be here today? Her aunt's reaction made her curious.

"I want you to be the one to wear the necklace today, Aunt Bertie. If my mother was here, I'm sure she'd agree. Besides, I have a feeling you're going to be lucky today."

Her aunt gazed wistfully at the necklace. "If you think so, dear."

"I do, and I mean every word," Melinda answered and kissed her aunt on her cheek. "Now go on and make yourself even more beautiful than you are right now. I'll be down for my own dress as soon as I take a hot bath."

Alone in the bathroom, Melinda glanced at the

closed door to make sure she was alone. She opened a brightly wrapped gift box she'd received at the shower and searched inside for the jars of decadent bath oils. She hadn't thought to use them so soon, if at all, but if she ever needed pampering and a mental lift, today was the day. She filled the tub, sprinkled in drops of scented oil and gingerly sank into the heated water.

Maybe because it was her frame of mind, but true to the mental and sensual euphoria advertised on the jars, an image of a too handsome, too sexy and too-sure-of-himself Ben Howard flashed across her mind. A man, her aunt Bertie had assured her and everyone within earshot at the shower, Melinda was destined to marry.

If only he wasn't so damn attractive, she thought wistfully. If only she wasn't drawn to the downright male sexual appeal that had her hormones dancing. If only she could stop visualizing herself in his arms and expressing the love she felt for him. And if only she could rely on Ben's promise to wait for her to call the shots in their relationship.

On the other hand, maybe she *could* rely on Ben's good intentions. Maybe the real problem was herself. How could she force *herself* to keep her part of the agreement when she ached to be held in his arms and loved until she wasn't able to think at all.

She wasn't fooling herself. The sexual tension between them wasn't all Ben's doing. It was more that his innate sensual attraction was strong and her resistance weak.

To complicate matters, there was the report of the

shower Martha Ebbetts had written. The small news-paper, largely devoted to local news, had carried the headline Destiny in bold print on the front page! Martha Ebbetts, at her romantic best, had even quoted Ben's tongue-in-cheek comment that it had been love at first sight! She could hide in the bridal shop, but Ben was a prominent businessman. What kind of ribbing was he taking?

If the article had embarrassed her, she could imagine what it would do to Ben. Biology apart, if he'd been upset with her before, there was no telling how he felt about her now.

She washed her hair, rinsed off and rubbed her hair dry until each strand gleamed. Glancing around the ancient, utilitarian bathroom, she visualized the private bathroom with gleaming gold fixtures at Ben's house. If she knew anything about his one-track mind and determined nature, he was surely in the process of turning the room into a his-and-hers bathroom.

Then there was the bedroom next to Ben's that she'd agreed to redecorate in a weak moment. Unless she was off target, the his-and-hers bedrooms would surely be transformed into a spacious master bedroom if he had his way.

All for a bride who wouldn't be a real bride.

If they had to live together for appearance's sake, she should have chosen a bedroom farther down the hall where she had privacy. And insisted on being able to lock the door from the inside.

The loud sound of the front door knocker downstairs drew her out of her reverie. Another wedding present? A corner of the bridal shop was already stacked with gifts that would have to be returned as soon as decently possible.

There was a polite knock on the bathroom door. "Your bridal bouquet has arrived, dear!"

Melinda hurriedly recapped her fantasy. The bouquet she'd ordered on the Internet! What next? She wrapped the robe around her and opened the door.

"What a happy choice," her aunt commented as she handed Melinda the bouquet. "It's a perfect match for your dress. I have a smaller one just like it."

Melinda gazed down at the nosegay of pink and white roses and delicate ferns nestled in a lacy doily. Matching pink ribbons trailed from the stems to her knees. Through its cellophane covering, she could see the accompanying package of the pink roses she'd ordered to wear in her hair.

"I pressed your dress for you and brought it up. Now, if you don't mind, I think I'll go get my own dress ready." Her aunt gestured to the closet and was out of the door before Melinda could thank her.

The three-quarter-length, sheer white slip-dress and its jacket embroidered with tiny pink roses that she'd described in her Internet wedding fantasy hung from the closet door. With the dress available in the bridal shop's inventory, at least there would be one less bill to face.

Melinda gazed at the dress and wondered if she could get through the wedding, let alone her wedding night. The thought made her head swim and her mouth turn dry.

A noise outside drew her to the open window. To

her dismay, wedding guests were already arriving at the park across the street. From the activity, it looked as if everyone who had nothing better to do on a Saturday afternoon was arriving to attend her wedding!

She thought hard and drew a blank. She hadn't sent any wedding invitations! Had the wedding announcement in the newspaper been an open invitation to the ceremony! Nor had she ordered the folding chairs being delivered. Were they the few items Zoe was apparently taking care of? What else had she forgotten?

She shivered, afraid to even think of what else Zoe would come up with next. Or what Ben would say when he saw the wedding arrangements mushrooming out of sight.

The only bright spot in the burgeoning wedding fiasco was that the Happy-Ever-After Bridal Attire Company had agreed to consider postponing the honeymoon rail trip award while they and Bertie renegotiated the large order she'd placed.

RITCHIE BURST into Ben's bedroom, his hair windblown and his white jacket open. "You're never going to believe it!"

Ben swore and stopped fussing with a bow tie that wouldn't lay straight. Too bad he'd already sent Manuel off to the wedding. "Believe what?"

"Half the town is fighting its way into Sunlight Park! When I drove by, I swear there must have been a dozen people jockeying for seats!"

"Get outahere," Ben snorted. "Melinda assured me she set up a small, intimate wedding in the park."

"I kid you not. As far as I could tell, there's standing room only!"

Ben frowned into the mirror. No matter how hard he tried, the damn black bow tie kept turning up crooked. "Are you sure they're there for the wedding? Tomorrow is July fourth. Maybe they're getting together for an early public holiday."

"No sir," Ritchie said gleefully. "I swear there's a path in the park that's cordoned off with white ribbon. Hell, there's even a red carpet leading from Miss Bertie's Bridal Shop to the park!"

"No way!" Ben retorted. "Why would Melinda invite so many guest when she…" He stopped short of admitting he'd had to persuade Melinda to go through with the wedding ceremony. If the answer was that she'd lost her mind, he'd have to tell her that when she found it she'd have to check for his.

"When she what?" Ritchie looked too interested.

"Never mind." Ben gave up on his tie. "Here, help me on with my jacket and we'll go find out just what's going on."

By the time Ben and Ritchie drove by, the street in front of the bridal shop had been cordoned off. No Parking signs had been placed around the perimeter of the park. People were milling around trying to find a free chair, bench or large rock to sit on. A few were sitting on blankets! Ben looked up at the clear, blue sky, half expecting to see the Goodyear blimp floating overhead trailing a sign with his name on it.

"I'll be damned if I'm going to wait for Melinda

out there in front of all those people," Ben finally muttered, his face grim. "Drive around the back. There's got to be a back door or a delivery entrance to the house."

To his relief, there was a small cement parking area. He strode into the kitchen, Ritchie hot on his heels.

"Benjamin Howard, you can't come in here!" Zoe hurried to block his entrance. "It's bad luck to see the bride in her wedding dress before the ceremony!"

"Hell…er, sorry, Miss Zoe," Ben answered. Since he towered over the petite woman, he had no problem looking over her shoulder. "I've got to find a place to hide until the ceremony. Besides, I have to talk to Melinda!"

"She's busy getting ready, young man. If you haven't spoken to her by now, it will have to wait. I'm afraid the best I can do for you is to find her aunt. Stay right here in the kitchen," she admonished with a stern look. "I'll be right back."

"Women!" Ritchie began. He swallowed his comment when Ben shot him a warning look. "Okay, so what are we going to do while we wait?"

Ben was too busy pacing the kitchen and muttering to himself to reply. Ritchie shrugged and reached for Bertie's famous cookie jar. Trays of cellophane-wrapped cookies waited beside it. "Not a bad way to pass the time," he said between bites. "Not bad at all."

Ben glanced at the cookie jar. "Yeah, right. When all else fails, try one of Ms. Bertie's cookies, I always say. How about giving me one."

By the time Bertie arrived, breathless and all aflutter, the two men had eaten halfway through the cookie jar.

"Benjamin, dear. Zoe says you sounded terribly upset!"

"Upset!" Ben wiped off his chin with the back of his hand and shook cookie crumbs off his white jacket. "That's putting it mildly, Ms. Bertie. Do you realize half of Ojai must be out there waiting for me to get married?" He glanced at his wristwatch. "And I'm not so sure the other half won't arrive by the time the ceremony is scheduled to begin!"

"Well, yes," she answered happily. "I'm afraid the wedding announcement and the article about the shower in the *Ojai Newsday* about your shower has whetted many a prospective bride's appetite. They may even start a new trend for weddings." She brushed a few remaining crumbs off of Ben's jacket and patted his shoulder. "But don't worry, dear. Zoe tells me she's called for police protection."

Ben closed his eyes and ran a damp hand across his forehead. "Police protection! What next?"

"Say," Ritchie suddenly commented before he started in on another cookie, "isn't there a law about how long and how many people can congregate in one place?"

Ben glowered at him. "Not in an open park. I think you're referring to parking on the street."

"Oh dear." Bertie darted a look at the trays of cookies waiting to be served to the wedding guests. "I don't think I've baked enough cookies for the reception!"

Ritchie looked expectant. "What else are you serving, Ms. Bertie?"

She hesitated and started for the pantry. "Melinda took care of the food, but I'm not sure there'll be enough cookies for everyone."

Wedding reception, be damned! As far as Ben was concerned, uninvited guests deserved to share only what food was available. To add to the problem, he was half afraid Bertie was going to put on an apron and start up a new batch of cookies. There was only one way he knew to stop her.

"Do you know how beautiful you look in that dress, Ms. Bertie? You look positively radiant. Doesn't she, Ritch?"

"You bet!"

Bertie stopped in mid-stride and turned back to Ben. "Do you really think so?"

"I do," he answered adamantly as he circled her where she stood. He'd fudged the truth. She had a pink rose in her upswept hair and looked years younger. Maybe it was the pink taffeta dress and the blush pearl necklace that took years off her age. Or was it that smile of pleasure that made her look so young? "Pink certainly becomes you. You're going to be the star attraction this afternoon."

"Oh no, dear boy. The bride is always the star attraction."

"Maybe so," he agreed. "But I've never seen you look happier, either. Not even when my high school basketball team won the pennant."

She dimpled at his praise. "I remember you claimed it was the cookies I'd baked for the team that gave them that extra push to win. In either case, you do know how to make an old woman happy.''

"Not so old, Ms. Bertie. Heck, my Uncle Joseph has to be a few years older than you are, and yet he looks great, too.''

The smile faded from her face. A strange, dreamy look replaced it before she shook her head. "What was it you wanted to see Melinda about?''

Ritchie cleared his throat. Ben motioned him into silence. "To tell you the truth, I'm not quite sure. I was going to read her the riot act about what's going on outside in the park, but...'' He shrugged and thought of Zoe. "On second thought, maybe Melinda's not to blame after all.''

"I knew I could count on you, dear boy,'' Bertie replied. She reached up to pat his cheek. "I'd like to kiss my new nephew, if it's all right with you?''

Ben leaned down so they were at eye level and smiled into her eyes. "I'd be mighty proud if you did, Ms. Bertie.''

"And a good-luck hug to send you on your way?''

"Definitely a hug,'' he agreed and opened his arms to her slight figure. "I need all the good luck wishes I can get.''

"Go on,'' she dimpled. "You were born under a lucky star.''

"How do you know that, Ms. Bertie?''

She smiled and touched her finger to her lips. "I just know.''

The bell in the church steeple on the other side of the park began to toll.

Ben silently counted to twelve before he heard a

flurry of activity coming from the stairway in the hall. Melinda! If it was bad luck to see a bride in her wedding dress before the ceremony, he didn't intend to wait around to find out. No matter what strange ideas Melinda had about love and lovemaking, she deserved the very best. The least he could do for her was to give her the chance. "Come on, Ritch. The wedding is about to start."

Chapter Nine

Ben squared his shoulders and made for the front door. It was no time for questions or second thoughts. He'd come this far, and there was no turning back. The last thing he wanted to do was spook the bride when she might be having last-minute second thoughts. He didn't need to create any more problems for himself than he already had.

He froze in his tracks when he reached the porch. He'd hadn't stopped to take a good look at what was going on out front, but Ritchie had been right.

Before his incredulous gaze, a red carpet started at the foot of the wooden stairs and stretched across the street to the park's main entrance. There, it met a pathway lined with flowering gardenia bushes adorned with white ribbons. As if that weren't enough to send his mind reeling, wedding guests were pouring into the park where a delivery service was unfolding white wooden chairs. A caterer's truck was delivering what appeared to be box lunches.

Seeing might be believing, but he found it hard to believe the fairy-tale fantasy unfolding in front of him. If this was Melinda's idea of a small, intimate wedding, what would her idea of a full-blown church affair have been?

"Jeez, I've got to be dreaming!" Ritchie's awed voice came over his shoulder. "Not even some of the royal weddings on television looked anything like this!"

Ben couldn't bear to contemplate what might come next. But if all this activity was Melinda's doing, he had no choice. He had to go along with her, even when he felt like a fool.

"I wonder who's paying for all of this? It must cost a bundle!" Ritchie's awed question echoed Ben's own thoughts.

A bundle was right, Ben agreed silently. Only not the kind Ritchie was talking about. Ritchie's idea of a bundle had dollar signs written all over it. *This* bundle had to involve the wedding gowns Bertie must have bartered in return for the overblown romantic wedding ambience. How Melinda would be able to talk their way out of her aunt's barter agreements, was anyone's guess.

Trading good-natured banter with a local policeman stationed at the foot of the stairs, Ben started for the park. The law had chocolate-chip cookie addict written all over him. Either he'd volunteered for duty or Bertie had bribed him. But why police? Unless someone was planning something *really* big.

Ben was beginning to feel he was caught in a romantic fantasy with no way out.

He counted twenty gardenia bushes as he strode toward the center of the park. Heated by the heavy noon sun, the scent of gardenias was overpowering. One bush would have been bad enough, but twenty? Twenty bushes tied with white ribbons! Surely, not even a romantic Melinda could possibly have dreamed all this up!

He took a good look at the gazebo. Decorated with pink roses, ferns and white ribbons, the structure resembled a large floral arrangement. Impossible! Melinda had explained she'd chosen the park to avoid costly florist's bills.

Bertie at work again?

He started up the steps where Dexter Rankin, his thespian friend from his Boston collegiate days, stood waiting for him.

"Thank goodness you're here," Ben murmured as they shook hands. "For a minute back there, I didn't know what to expect if you didn't turn up. Or," he added, "what you might turn up with."

Dex smiled broadly. "A choir? If you want me to try, I'm sure there's some singers in the crowd."

"No way!" With an incredulous look around him, Ben shuddered. "I was afraid you weren't going to get here in time for the ceremony. Although, the way things are going, nothing would surprise me."

Dex grinned and, with a glance at their audience, pretended to bless Ben. "I wasn't sure I was going to make it here on time, myself. That's why I told you I'd make my own flight arrangements. I have a performance tomorrow afternoon, so I'll have to catch a red-eye tonight."

"Glad to hear it, but don't overdo the clerical bit," Ben cautioned under his breath. "There's a pro in the

front seat.'' He nodded pleasantly at the Reverend
Charles Good.

The good reverend already looked suspicious. Ben
couldn't blame him. He didn't know where Dex had
rented his ''costume,'' but the white satin robe didn't
look like anything Ben had seen before. If there had
been wings attached, the guy would have looked like
an oversized angel. ''Do me a favor, Dex.''

''Anything for an old friend.''

''Just try to remember this is an ecumenical ceremony,'' Ben cautioned under his breath. ''And, for
Pete's sake, keep it brief.''

''Got it!'' Dex agreed cheerfully. He looked over
Ben's shoulder. ''So, where's the bride?''

Ben checked the doorway to the house across the
street. Melinda should have been on her way by
now—had she gotten cold feet at the last minute?
''She'll show up any minute now,'' he answered,
more to reassure himself than his thespian friend.
''Melinda prides herself on being on time.''

He turned around to introduce Ritchie, but the guy
was in deep conversation with a tall, gangly young
man dressed in a tuxedo whose trousers were miles
too short for him. The kid held a flute in his hand.
Ben felt relieved. At the rate things were going, there
could have been a small orchestra.

''I'd like you to meet my best man, Ritchie Morrison, but it looks as if he's busy at the moment.''

''Is he in on it?'' Dex whispered.

Ben shook his head. ''So far, it's just you, me and
Melinda. So play it straight.'' He searched the audience for his uncle. When he found him seated in the

middle of the crowd, he motioned him to move closer to a row marked Reserved for Family. No way was his uncle going to hide out at a time like this. Ben needed all the support he could get.

"There she is," someone in the crowd shouted. Ben snapped to attention and started down to the steps to meet his bride. The first person to appear in the doorway was a radiant Bertie. She was dressed in a pale-pink silk dress and carried a nosegay of tiny pink roses and maidenhair fern. Applause and whistles greeted her.

At Ben's side, the flutist, who Ben recognized as a member of the high school's basketball team and marching band that he sponsored, spat out his chewing gum and prepared to musically usher in the bride.

"I never thought you'd actually marry someone you met on a Web site, Mr. Howard," Tate Wilson laughed. "Way to go, man!"

Ben swung around to stare at him. "You what?"

The boy's face paled. "Can we talk about it later, Mr. Howard? Ms. Zoe says I have to be ready to play the wedding march when the bride comes out the door."

Ben resisted the urge to grab the kid and shake the whole Web site story out of him. A voice whispered: Don't kill the messenger just because you don't like the message. "Ms. Zoe arranged for you to be here?"

"Yeah. I heard she and Ms. Bertie lined up almost everything," he gestured to their surroundings. "Cool!"

Ben shuddered. "Including the red carpet? And the policeman?"

"I guess so." Tate took a step back at the growing look of dismay on Ben's face.

Ben regarded him skeptically. From what he'd been told, Zoe didn't have any more financial resources than Bertie.

"How much is she paying you?"

Tate attempted a grin. "A month's supply of chocolate-chip cookies."

"My God!" Ben exploded. "Are chocolate-chip cookies going to replace U.S. currency here in Ojai?"

This time the young man actually laughed. "Ms. Bertie is going to be the one who's paying off. Ms. Zoe says she doesn't even know how to cook."

"What!" Ben hissed in annoyance. The woman ran a tea shop and didn't know the first thing about cooking? What was going on here? No wonder the bridal shower had leaned heavily on dainty cucumber and watercress sandwiches.

Zoe didn't know the first thing about weddings, either, he mused darkly, or the park and its surroundings wouldn't look like something out of a fairy tale.

It wasn't the part about getting married that bothered him—he had his bases covered. It was the dozens of pairs of eyes that were watching him. And the strong possibility that, if Ritchie had had anything to do with it, they all knew about the picture on the dating Web site.

Another burst of applause kept him from wringing the whole truth out of the kid. "Okay for now, wise guy," he said in Tate's face, "but this conversation isn't over. I intend to find out what you're talking about. And, if it's what I think it is…"

In the interest of leaving the kid enough breath to play the wedding march, he left the threat unfinished. "And remember, if you don't find me after the ceremony, I'll find you!"

His Adam's apple bobbing while he tried to swallow, the boy nodded his agreement. Ben gave him a firm look and turned away.

Bertie, Melinda's maid-of-honor, had reached the first gardenia bush and was about to head down the path to where Ben was waiting. Sunshine enveloped her in a radiant glow. Dressed in that pink taffeta dress with matching roses in her hair, she looked lovely and younger than he'd ever seen her before.

The flutist started playing. A chorus of oohs and aahs followed Melinda's aunt as she made her way up the path. She'd almost reached his side when she stopped and turned to look at someone in the front row of seated spectators. A hush fell over the audience. The flutist hesitated. For a minute, it seemed as if the world had stopped, or at least gone into slow motion.

Ben craned his neck to see who or what had drawn Bertie's attention.

She was gazing off to her left. Her smile, if radiant before, became even more luminous. To his surprise, she nodded to someone seated in the audience.

Ben saw his Uncle Joseph put fingers to his lips. To Ben's amazement, Bertie acknowledged the gesture with a shy nod and continued on her way toward Ben.

His uncle, whom he assumed knew Bertie but not

that intimately, had blown her a kiss? It was a scene out of a romantic movie.

Uncle Joseph? Bertie?

Wheels began to turn in Ben's mind. Starting with his photograph on the Internet followed by Melinda's "little mistake" on her computer, there were too many coincidences for him to ignore. He began to think he'd been set up.

What was clear was that his uncle and Melinda's aunt knew each other. Just how well and how involved they were in events that were ending here at an altar in a public park was something he intended to find out.

He went down the remaining step and held out his arm for Bertie to take. "Ready?"

She took a deep breath. The smile she bestowed on Ben put the sun to shame. "Very ready, Benjamin."

He escorted her up the few steps into the gazebo and wondered just what his about-to-be aunt was ready for.

There was another burst of applause. The audience turned as one to look at the bride who stood on the porch across the street. The flutist went back into action. Ben headed back down the steps.

Melinda's three-quarter-length white silk dress and short jacket embroidered with tiny pink flowers hugged a figure fit for a goddess. Her shoes were white. The nosegay she carried was made of pink and white roses with a white orchid in the center. Her blond hair was caught up and held by a tiara of pink roses.

The effect was breathtaking. But Ben's thoughts

flew back to the time her hair had been loose and flying in the wind. He wondered what the chances were that he would ever see it spread across a white pillow for him to admire.

He thought again of the promise he'd made to let Melinda call the shots in their relationship. The chances of him ever finding out looked slim to none.

He watched in admiration as his bride-to-be crossed the red carpet and started up the gardenia-scented path. She didn't need any wedding finery to make her look beautiful, he thought proudly. Her beauty came from within. Like her aunt, she was compassionate, caring and generous. Otherwise, she wouldn't be marrying him, would she?

His thoughts, far from platonic, turned to the probability of happy days and nights. Until he noticed that Melinda seemed reluctant.

It was the way she walked. Where her aunt's steps had been sure, Melinda's were hesitant. Where her aunt had looked radiant, Melinda looked apprehensive. He'd believed he'd convinced her they were doing the right thing. Now, he wasn't so sure.

Melinda's thoughts as she walked up the path to where Ben's actor friend waited to "marry" them, were in a turmoil.

From the day she'd been old enough to envy the brides being fitted for their wedding gowns in her aunt's shop, she'd dreamed of becoming a bride herself. At nine, the mental image of her groom had been hazy. The only really attractive men she'd seen were actors in movies, and she was smart enough to know they didn't count.

Then came the first time she'd seen Ben Howard in action on the high school basketball court. Tall and lean, arm and chest muscles firm and taut from years of shooting basketball hoops, he'd been every teenage girl's dream. The first time he'd brushed his tawny hair away from his eyes and flashed his famous victory grin, he'd stolen her heart away.

Not that he'd noticed her. He had more girls swooning over him than any one boy was entitled to.

It wasn't until she was a junior and Ben a senior that she'd mustered up enough nerve to choose him for a partner at a high school dance. The same arms that had shot baskets had held her and taught her how to disco. The same brown eyes had teased and laughed down at her. She'd been smitten more than ever, but she'd never had the impression he was actually *seeing* her. Certainly not in the way he was looking at her now.

She'd never forgotten Ben in intervening years. Not even when she'd heard from her aunt that he'd married and divorced a girl his last year in college.

Finding him on a dating Web site had been a shock. Choosing him as her fantasy bridegroom had been a mistake. Finding herself about to marry the man of her dreams was hard to accept.

Not when their marriage was going to be a marriage of convenience entered into for someone else's benefit. And not when she knew Ben intended to dissolve the marriage as soon as decently possible.

Would her future be like Bertie's? Living on dreams of what might have been?

When she reached Ben, he took her hand in his. Concern showed in his eyes. "Are you okay?"

Afraid she'd given herself away, she nodded.

"For a minute there, I was getting a little worried," he answered with a relieved smile. "You looked as if you were going to cut and run."

She looked up into his eyes. "Would you care if I did?"

"Of course, I'd care." He gave her his arm to escort her up the stairs where his friend waited to marry them. "What makes you think I wouldn't? We both agreed we have a lot riding on this ceremony, right?"

It wasn't the answer she longed to hear. "I'm not sure," she answered helplessly. "Weddings always make me a little crazy." How could she give him an intelligent answer when she didn't know the answer herself? How could she have wanted him for a fantasy husband and still not be sure she was ready to marry him now?

Still, she thought in despair, he was right about there being a lot riding on their marriage.

They mounted the last step and reached the "minister." The flutist ended the wedding march with a flourish and faded behind a potted palm. The best man was grinning from ear to ear, but her maid-of-honor kept glancing into the audience. Melinda tried to take a firmer grip on herself.

"Shall we begin?" the "minister" inquired politely.

Bertie reached for Melinda's bridal nosegay and gave her an encouraging smile.

The best man searched in his coat pocket for the wedding ring.

Melinda stared blankly at the minister.

"We are," Ben said firmly. He reached for her cold right hand and rubbed it between his. "Everything is going to be all right," he whispered to her. "I promise."

Which promise did Ben intend to keep, Melinda thought fleetingly. A short, platonic marriage? And how all right would that be?

"In that case…" The minister cast a wary eye at Melinda and opened a book of prayers.

"Dear friends, we are gathered here to join this man and this woman in holy matrimony…"

At the sound of the ministers words "holy matrimony" Melinda's heart went into a tailspin. She'd never been a particularly religious person, but the opening words of the marriage ceremony held a deep meaning for her. Marriage *was* a holy sacrament.

No! No! a voice in her head shrieked. *You can't do this! You can't!*

The realization that there wouldn't have been anything sacred in a marriage to her erstwhile fiancé had been largely the reason she'd left San Francisco. Regardless of Ben's earlier marital experience, she felt vows made during the ceremony were a promise of a lifelong commitment. A make-believe ceremony, annulment or divorce only made a mockery of her own beliefs.

A murmur rose from the wedding guests.

Melinda realized the minister had asked her a question and was waiting for an answer. If he'd performed the earlier part of the marriage ceremony, she hadn't heard it. There had been decisions to make.

"Do you, Melinda Susan Carey, take this man, Benjamin Foster Howard for your husband?" the minister repeated slowly. Clearly, the man had repeated a question he must have asked at least once before. "To have and to hold in sickness and in health from this day forward?" He waited expectantly while Melinda glanced up at Ben.

A frown creased Ben's forehead, the expression in his eyes watchful. His grip on her hand tightened.

The minister coughed.

Her conscience told her to say yes—she'd come this far and she ought to see it through. Her problem was that her tongue didn't seem to be able to form the words "I do."

And if she did, would Ben promise to love, honor and cherish her in return? An empty promise, at best.

How could she commit to an empty marriage of convenience when the years were passing so swiftly? If she did, would she ever have a real marriage and the family she longed for?

The minister cleared his throat and started to repeat the question. Melinda shook her head. She didn't want to hurt Ben, but she couldn't go through with the ceremony. If destiny had brought her and Ben together, there must have been some mistake. It had chosen the wrong man and woman.

The minister waited. Her aunt whispered her encouragement. The best man began to whistle under his breath.

Melinda knew she was about to break her aunt's

heart, but she couldn't help herself. She wasn't a young girl anymore, dreaming dreams of knights in shining armor or mooning over handsome movie stars. Or picking impossibly attractive men off the Internet for a husband—real or not.

It was time to let go of dreams, to grow up. There had to be another way to solve her problems.

She imagined she could hear the sound of her own heart breaking. Ben didn't look too happy, either. She took a firm grip on herself—it was better to correct a wrong now before it was too late.

"I'm sorry." She took her hand out of Ben's. "My answer has to be no."

"No?" Ben reached for her again. "Melinda! You can't mean it. Not now!"

"I'm afraid I do." She turned to the minister. "Thank you for coming, Mr. Rankin. I'm sorry to have put you to so much trouble. And you too, Aunt Bertie," she added softly. "I know how much this meant to you."

"Any chance I can persuade you to reconsider?" Ben spoke slowly, but his heart was racing at the thought of losing Melinda. Any lingering doubts that she'd been in on setting him up on the Internet faded. No way would she have purposefully make a laughing stock out of herself or her aunt. And that's exactly what would happen if she left him at the altar.

He couldn't let her do it. Not without trying one last time. He wanted her in his life and in the rooms he intended to redecorate for her. Without her, he realized with a pang of regret, the house would be empty—as would his heart. More rode on her answer than he'd realized.

"I promised you everything would work out okay in the end, Melinda, and I meant it. Just say yes. We can talk about what's bothering you later."

"I can't. Maybe at another time and place destiny might have worked. But not now. Not when I've finally realized okay isn't enough."

In the background their audience began to react to the stalled ceremony. "What's going on up there?" someone shouted. A number of guests stood to get a better view. The policeman watching from the rear of the crowd started forward.

"I'm sure it's only a case of stage fright, dear," her aunt said worriedly. "Maybe if you took a deep breath, we could start over. Don't you think so, Reverend?"

"Stage fright," Dex agreed. "I remember it well. I don't mind starting over."

Melinda shook her head.

"Are you sure?" her aunt urged. "I'm sure Benjamin is willing. It's not too late."

Melinda took a deep breath and started to turn away. "No, Aunt Bertie, it's never too late to do the right thing. I'll call Martha Ebbetts tomorrow and explain my mistake."

"No way!" Ben exploded. He reached for her. "You might not want to go through with this, but you're not going to share the details with that woman! By the time she gets through spreading the news, your aunt might as well close the bridal shop. It was for her sake that this whole thing started, remember?"

Melinda remembered. Too well. And felt worse than ever. "I'm sorry, I still can't go through with this."

Tears rose in her eyes at the thought this might be the last time she and Ben would speak. And how much she would miss him, if it were. He might have insisted they go through with the charade, but it *had* been her idea in the first place.

"You're sure?"

"I'm sure."

"Okay, have it your way," Ben said grimly. "But you're not going to drag your name—and your aunt's—through the mud. Not if I can help it."

"What did you have in mind?" Ritchie inquired, gesturing to the park where some of the guests had risen and started for the gazebo.

"I'm going to take the fall for this." Ben reached to brush away a tear from Melinda's flushed cheek. Impulsively, he leaned over and kissed her tenderly. "I regret the way this is turning out, Melinda. It's my fault for insisting. I talked you into going through with this fool stunt even though I'd already realized you'd thought the better of it. Maybe you were right, after all."

"I'm so sorry," she said again. "It's my fault, too. I should have called the whole thing off before we got this far."

"Maybe, but you're not going to get hurt by this, either." Ben took a deep breath and regarded her tenderly. "If anyone asks, just tell them I was the one who changed his mind and left you at the altar. But I want you to know this isn't over. I'll see you later." He turned to his best man. "Come on, Ritch, let's get out of here."

Chapter Ten

"What the hell was that all about?" Ritchie panted behind him.

"Later," Ben said tersely over his shoulder. "I've got to get out of here." He made for the safety of the house across the street.

Mouths agape, curious spectators stood when Ben strode by, Ritchie at his heels. There was the buzz of excited speculation and a few snide remarks. A newspaper photographer snapped his picture.

Shielding his face from the camera with his elbow, Ben kept going as if the devil was at his heels.

Out of the corner of his eye, he caught a glimpse of Melinda helping her aunt down the gazebo steps. Not to his surprise, his uncle had appeared and was reaching for Bertie. He mentally thanked her for diverting his uncle's attention.

Ben grit his teeth. As much as he wanted to wait in the bridal shop for Melinda and talk over their future, he was in no mood to face his uncle. He might be fresh out of answers, but he was mad as hell. And the asinine thing about it all, was that he was angry at himself for putting himself and Melinda in harm's way.

He'd told himself the wedding fantasy was a game. He'd been wrong. The game they'd agreed to play had become real and hurtful.

"Get the car, Ritch," he said over his shoulder. "I'm going home. I need to think."

Ritch hung back. "What about Josie? She's going to want to know what happened back there. And so do I!"

"Josie will keep. I have a few things to figure out for myself and I don't need an audience. Coming?"

"Yeah, sure. But I saw her heading this way and I didn't like the look on her face. Go on. I'll catch up with you in a minute."

"Make it quick!" Ben headed for the parking lot at the back of the house.

The policeman guarding the red carpet snapped to attention as Ben passed. He darted a look over Ben's shoulder at the crowd milling around the gazebo. "Problems, Mr. Howard?"

"None that I can't handle. Thanks," Ben called over his shoulder. He had to get out of here and he wasn't going to let anything or anyone stop him. Not even when he knew he was going to be the hot topic of conversation in Ojai.

Hell, what was the use of trying to explain, anyway? From the way the crowd was milling around back in the park, there wouldn't be a soul in Ojai who wouldn't think of him as a scoundrel. Not that he didn't care what people thought of him, he did. More than he ever thought he would. He just couldn't afford to care right now.

"Hey, Howard!" A strident voice called behind him. The news photographer was striding around the house, his camera pointed at Ben. To Ben's relief, Ritchie sprinted past him and slid into the driver's seat.

"Let's get out of here!"

"I will as soon as I find the damn car keys," Ritchie said between gasps for air.

"What did you tell Josie?"

"Not much," Ritchie panted. "The last I saw her, she was heading for Melinda. By the way, Ms. Zoe wanted to know what she should tell the caterer. I told her to use her own best judgment."

Ben eyed the photographer warily. The guy was too close for comfort. "Good diversionary tactics. Let her handle it. That'll make one less person bending Melinda's ear."

Ritchie frantically searched his pockets again for the car keys. "So what's going on, or are you out of your mind?" He grimaced when he came up with Melinda's wedding ring. "What do you want me to do with this?"

Ben reached for the small gold circle and clenched it in his hand. How had he expected a woman like Melinda to say "I do" when her wedding vows were meant to be a lie?

The newspaper photographer leaned over the car's windshield, camera at the ready. "Hey, Howard! Hold up a minute! Where's the bride?"

Ben swore. "Let's go, Ritch!"

Ritchie turned on the motor and stepped on the gas. The determined photographer wound up against the windshield, still snapping pictures like crazy.

Gunning the car's motor, Ritchie looked up at the rearview mirror to where the photographer was picking himself up off the asphalt. "Thank God. I thought I killed the guy!"

"Hell," Ben groaned. He looked over his shoulder and shuddered. The photographer was still snapping pictures. "This is going to make one hell of a story."

"Could be worse," Ritchie answered. "I could have run over the guy." He took his eyes off the road long enough to peer at Ben. "So, tell me. Why couldn't you let Melinda do the walking?"

Ben rolled his eyes. It was a question he knew would be asked from now until eternity. He would have liked to keep the answer to himself, but as a player in this afternoon's farce, Ritchie was entitled to some kind of answer. "Because she was right and I was the one who was wrong."

Ritchie took his eyes off the road long enough to peer at Ben suspiciously. "How wrong?"

Ben shot him a disgusted look. "Not that wrong. I just never promised her the life she deserves to have. As if that wasn't bad enough, I wasn't the first guy to let her down. After her sorry experiences with men, she had no reason to trust any of us."

"Melinda's been married before?"

"No. Engaged." Ben loosened the top button of a shirt that had become too tight. "Melinda told me she lost her mother when she was eight. It didn't help matters when her father walked out on her and sent her to live with her aunt.''

"Tough," Ritchie agreed. "But living with Ms. Bertie couldn't have been all that bad."

"No. Her aunt is great." Ben silently faced the truth. "It's only the men in Melinda's life who hurt her. When I came into the picture, I didn't turn out to be an improvement," he added wryly. "I'm afraid I didn't give her any reason to trust me, either."

Ritchie eyed him warily and carefully steered through weekend traffic. "I don't know what happened, but Josie thinks the world of you. From what I hear, so do most of the women around here. It's just too bad you had to be the fall guy for the other men who let Melinda down."

Ben watched the orange groves drop behind them as they headed toward the hills. The air was scented by the orange blossoms synonymous with brides and weddings. Ben felt worse than ever. If only Melinda had been seated beside him instead of Ritchie and they were headed for their honeymoon night. If only he hadn't been such a jerk. He'd taken her harmless scheme, turned it into a travesty on love and marriage and broken her heart in the process. "I guess I had it coming. Anyway, I figured I can take the notoriety better than Melinda can."

Ritchie turned off on to the country road that led up to Ben's hilltop house. The miles of orange groves gave way to the flowering apricot orchards that were a portion of the source of Ben's Oak Tree brandies. "I don't know exactly what Melinda expected from you, but whatever was going on, she had to know you'd fallen for her." He glanced pointedly at Ben. "Maybe she cares for you more than she's willing to admit. Given a chance, I think the two of you would have had a chance to make it."

"So did I," Ben answered. "But somewhere along the line, I seem to have forgotten to let Melinda in on the secret. I let her think ours was just going to be a marriage of convenience, dissolved on request by either party."

Ritchie guffawed. "You make marriage sound like a business enterprise! No wonder Melinda decided to call the whole thing off. Still, if things hadn't worked out, she could have asked for a divorce."

"Melinda is the kind of woman who plays for keeps."

Ritchie took his eyes off the road long enough to send him a searching look. "And you're not?"

Ben felt more dejected than ever. "Beats me. I didn't think about it, not after my divorce. But I'm beginning to believe it now."

Ritchie puffed out his chest like a male pouter pigeon on the make. "Take it from me, I'm an expert on the subject. You gotta tell women you love 'em at least three times a day. And every night before they go to sleep."

Ritchie made it sound so simple. Maybe he was right. If all it took to make Melinda happy was to keep telling her he'd fallen in love with her, he should have given it a go. Maybe he would have been able to convince her he wanted a real marriage. With a real minister and a real honeymoon, and kids somewhere down the line.

The look Ritchie gave him suggested Ben was a fool. He was right about that, too. But when he bared his soul, it would be to Melinda.

"Anyway, the next time I ask Melinda to marry me, I'm going to do it right."

Incredulous, Ritchie laughed until he almost lost control of the car. Swearing under his breath, he steered back to the right side of the road. "What are you going to do again?"

"The whole marriage bit. I'm not giving up on Melinda. I'm going to court her the old-fashioned way. And this time, I'm going to convince her I'm not the hit-and-run type of guy. And when we get married, it's going to be for keeps."

Ritchie rolled his eyes. The car skidded to a stop with a screech of rubber on asphalt. "I can't take much more of this. The next time you need a best man, better make sure you're going to go through with the deal. And, by the way—" he gestured to the house "—you're home. I can't come inside. I have to find Josie and think of a reason why you ran out on Melinda. Just what, I'm not sure. As it is, she thinks you and I are ready for the loony bin."

"Maybe we are." Ben got out of the car and started toward the house. "With the way your devious mind works," he called, "I'm sure you'll think of something to tell her. Give her a hug for me. And, by the way—" he stopped and turned back "—thanks."

He stood watching as Ritchie sped along the spiral road that led down the hill. Ritchie had a diabolical mind and a sense of humor equal to the task. Good friend or not, he still considered the guy a prime suspect in the dating Web site caper. If his hunch turned out to be right, and he was willing to bet it was, he'd thank him for bringing Melinda into his life. And then he'd show him the error of his ways.

Manuel opened the door before he had a chance to use his keys. "I heard the car, Mr. Ben. Welcome home, Mrs.—" He glanced over Ben's shoulder at the empty portico. "No bride?"

"No bride," Ben echoed. He grit his teeth and strode into the house.

"Maybe later?"

"Yeah, maybe later," Ben agreed. He loosed his bow tie and shrugged off his jacket. "How come you're still here? I thought I gave you a couple of weeks off."

"I'm going to leave soon," Manuel answered politely. He gestured to an elaborate floral bouquet that graced the hall table. "I just stayed long enough to make everything comfortable and beautiful for your new wife. I also fixed a light supper for you and Mrs. Howard." Too polite to question the absence of Ben's bride, Manuel's gaze was bland.

The reality of the situation hit Ben like a truck hurtling through a brick wall. The ache in his gut became real and painful. Manuel might have outdone himself, Ben thought dejectedly, but there would be no wife to share the intimate supper. No wife to reminisce with about their wedding. No wife to break the deafening silence of the enormous house. And no wife to kiss good-night. Instead, he'd be spending what should have been his wedding night alone.

Ironically, he *had* planned to tell Melinda tonight

that he'd discovered how much he cared for her. That he was even growing to love her. Something had held him back, and now that he knew what the something was, things were going to change. The next time he saw Melinda, he'd lay all his cards out on the table.

Heaven help him, in spite of his brave words to Ritchie and the promises he'd made to himself to win over Melinda, he didn't know where to begin or how long that would take.

His mind whirling with possibilities, Ben headed up the stairs. The fact that his uncle hadn't shown up to question him was enough to tell Ben his uncle had remained with Bertie. Finding out just how well they knew each was going to be his second order of business.

The first would be to find the kid with the flute and to find out what he and Ritchie had been talking about before the failed wedding ceremony. From the expression on the kid's face, and the remark he'd made about Ben marrying someone he'd met on the Internet, the kid had to know how Ben's photograph got there.

Somewhere in between, he'd have to find the time to court Melinda.

He wandered down the hall to the room Melinda had chosen for herself. A faint scent of honeysuckle perfume clung to the luggage she'd sent on ahead and that Manuel had been too polite to unpack. He glanced around the silent room and tried to envision Melinda there beside him. All he could see was the tight expression on her face when she'd said she was sorry and refused to say the traditional "I do."

The thought of returning the suitcases to his missing bride became unbearable.

On the other hand, there was one way out, he mused. His spirits picked up. He could keep the luggage and make Melinda come for it. It was the one sure way to persuade her to listen to him on his home territory without any interruptions from her aunt or his uncle. Satisfied with having taken the first step in winning Melinda back, he reached for the bottle of champagne Manuel had left for him.

ACROSS THE OJAI valley, Melinda firmly closed and locked the door behind her aunt and her escort. She hadn't had the heart to tell him or her aunt she wanted to be alone. Not after the protective way he was holding her aunt's hand. And not after she saw the yellow rose he wore in his navy-blue jacket lapel. A sure sign he'd been the anonymous sender of the yellow roses a few days ago.

Tall and slender, with silver-gray hair curling at the nape of his neck, he looked like a gallant older version of the young man her aunt had described and whom she'd had fallen in love with years ago. From the way her aunt was gazing up at him, she was in love with him still.

More disquieting was his similarity to Ben. Even with the cleft in his chin and his sparkling blue eyes. Funny how she and her aunt had fallen in love with two versions of the same man.

"My name is Joseph Howard, Miss Carey. I hope I'm not intruding," he said, "but I felt you needed some support. And, for that matter," he added with a soft smile at her aunt, "Tildy, too."

A blush came over her aunt's face. The tender look they exchanged sent Melinda's heartbeat racing. If only Ben had looked at her in the way they were looking at each other, she would have been in his arms right now.

"You must be the one who sent the yellow roses to my aunt last week?"

"Yes," he grinned boyishly. "I'm also Ben's uncle."

Melinda thought of the bittersweet story her aunt had told her about the young man she'd loved and lost long ago. A glance at the way her aunt was looking at Joseph Howard told Melinda he was that man.

"Why come here now, after all those years?"

He turned to Melinda's aunt. "I know I owe you some kind of explanation, Tildy, but I'd hoped to tell it to you in private after Ben and your niece were married. But now—" he gestured to the clamor in the street outside the door "—I suppose I owe Melinda an explanation, too. Do you mind?"

Her aunt blushed a becoming shade of pink. "No, of course not. Why don't we go into the kitchen where we can sit and talk. I'll have coffee ready in a moment or two. And some of the cookies you used to like." At the droll look he gave her, she blushed again.

The scent of freshly baked cookies still lingered in the kitchen. Melinda had lost track of the many hundreds of chocolate-chip cookies her aunt had baked through the years. Now, Melinda knew why. Joseph Howard had once told her he liked them.

No wonder her aunt's cookies had become famous. She put her heart, soul and dreams into them.

"Sit down, Tildy," Ben's uncle said, his hand outstretched to draw her to him. "We can have coffee later. It's time for the three of us to talk." He studied Melinda for a long moment. "Why don't you have your aunt put your bridal bouquet in the refrigerator for now?"

To her surprise, Melinda discovered she was still clinging tightly to her wedding nosegay. "I don't need it anymore." She tossed it into the trash container at the side of the sink and slid into a chair. The knowing look he gave her made her realize he could read her broken heart. She had to tell him the truth before he came up with a reason why she and Ben should get married. And before he unjustly blamed Ben.

"Before you begin, Mr. Howard, I should tell you Ben told me about the bargain you struck with him if he married me." Her gaze challenged him to deny it.

"Bargain?" Her aunt inquired, her attention focused on Joseph. "What kind of bargain?"

"I told Ben I would transfer the Howard properties to him now if he married your niece."

Bertie's face turned white. The plate of cookies she held dropped to the floor with a thud. Broken crockery and cookies scattered. "You bribed Ben to marry Melinda?"

"No! I made my intentions known *after* I'd read

he and Melinda were engaged to be married.'' Anxiously, he jumped up and led Melinda's aunt to a chair. ''We can sweep that up later.'' He turned back to Melinda. ''The fact is, Ben has been independently wealthy for many years. And more so since he started the brandy distillery. He doesn't need the Howard properties. I was the one who wanted him to have them.''

''Then why…?'' Bertie's hands fluttered to her lips. Tears threatened in her eyes.

''Because I thought Ben needed to be married, Tildy. To have a loving wife and children. I didn't want him to be alone and lonely the way I was after I lost Martha.'' He gathered her cold hands in his and gently stroked them. ''I knew what a wonderful woman you are, Tildy. And once I read the newspaper announcement, I wanted Ben to marry a woman who was the niece of the lovely woman I'd admired for many years.''

Tears formed in her aunt's eyes. He wiped her tears away with a gentle forefinger. ''Please don't cry. It's true. I have admired you, Tildy. For what it's worth, that year I was home on holiday, I was too young and too self-absorbed to tell you how much I did like you. More than that, I was too young to understand what love meant.''

He glanced apologetically at Melinda, then turned back to Bertie. ''You'll have to forgive an old man his memories, my dear.''

''Why didn't you come home when you graduated from college, Mr. Howard? You must have known my aunt had fallen in love with you.''

"I'm afraid I got sidetracked. I eventually fell in love with and married the daughter of a family friend back in Boston. We remained there for many years; until I came home to claim my own inheritance. Ben did much the same thing, but he wasn't as lucky in his marriage as I was."

Bertie started to speak, but he held his finger to her lips. "Don't mistake me, Tildy. I loved Martha and was a faithful husband until she passed away a few years ago."

"Oh, Joseph." Melinda's aunt patted his hand and fought back tears. "You don't have to convince me. I've seen the two of you together many times, you know. I'm sure you made her very happy."

"I hope so," he sighed. "Unfortunately, we never had children of our own. Now there's only Ben to carry on the Howard name and traditions. That's why I made him the proposition. Who better to help him carry them on than your niece?"

Melinda stirred uneasily as her own memories flooded in. Ben's quirky smile when he'd invited her on a picnic. The sensuous longing in his eyes as he kissed her. The taste of him, the scent of him, the sound of his voice murmuring terms of endearment. And the way she'd longed to become part of him.

Enveloped in the warmth of his gaze, she'd been tempted to do more than return his kisses. Until she realized she couldn't live with herself. How could she make love with him when he'd never told her he cared for her? Even after she'd shown him how much she cared for him? She'd asked to be taken home, even though every nerve ending in her body had clamored for her to stay and become his.

She returned Joseph's searching look. Her loyalty to Ben kept her from blurting out the truth that, had they married, Ben would have been her husband in name only, and at his suggestion. And that if Ben *had* cared for her, she would have been proud to be his wife and mother of his children. But Ben hadn't asked.

"Your aunt has told me that you were the one who actually called the wedding off, Melinda," Joseph went on. "And that my nephew chose to do it to spare you any gossip. He was right. Now it's my turn to help. Is there anything I can do to persuade you to change your mind?"

"No, thank you, Mr. Howard," Melinda said proudly. "Just make my aunt happy."

"I'm going to try," he agreed with a loving glance at Bertie. Her eyes were filled with happy tears. "I didn't realize how much I wanted to until I read your wedding announcement in the newspaper. From that moment on, the two weeks we spent together all those years ago became as fresh as though they'd happened yesterday." He cleared his throat and turned back to Melinda. "I confess that the announcement served a dual purpose. After reading it, I decided that if you were anything like Tildy, I wanted you for a niece. If your aunt is willing, I'd be proud to pick up where we left off."

Melinda's own tears threatened to spill over when she saw the blinding smile come over her aunt's face. "If you want my blessing, you have it. But as for

Ben, that's another story. I'm willing to admit my mistake in involving him in my wedding fantasy, but it's over.''

"Wedding fantasy?''

Melinda forced a smile. "It's a long story. Aunt Bertie can tell you about it later. But you should know there's never been anything between Ben and me. Except for my imagination.'' She stood and took the circle of roses out of her hair. "Now if you'll excuse me, I have to change.''

"Somehow I think there's more between you than that,'' Joseph said reflectively. "I know my nephew, maybe better than he knows himself. He's a very determined young man. He not only works hard to get where he wants, he doesn't give up easily.''

His smile sent waves of excitement running through Melinda.

NOTNG THAT THE fourth of July was only days away, and that the high school band would be performing, Ben began looking for Tate at band practice. He watched silently from the sidelines as the Nordhoff High School band marched in formation across the playing field. It came as no surprise to him to note that Tate had two left feet.

Ben signaled the bandleader and pointed to the gangly flute player. When the man nodded, Ben moved to take Tate by the elbow and lead him off the field.

"Gee, Mr. Howard,'' the boy protested. "I swear I looked for you after the wedding. There was so much confusion I couldn't see you. But I was going to look for you today after practice, honest.''

"Sure, you were," Ben agreed. "This won't take but a minute."

Tate looked appealingly at the band master over his shoulder. When he realized no help was forthcoming, he gave in. "What did you want to know?"

"How you knew about my being on the Internet, for one. And what Mr. Morrison knew about it, for another." Ben kept his voice even, a smile on his face. But sure as hell the kid got the message.

"I don't know anything about Mr. Morrison, but all the guys were talking about it," Tate answered with a feeble grin. It faded when Ben snorted his opinion.

"What guys?"

Tate looked around for help. When none was forthcoming, he answered. "I don't remember."

"Like hell! And who put the photograph there? You?"

Tate took a step backward. "Gosh, no, Mr. Howard. I wouldn't do such a thing! Honest!"

"But you think it's funny?"

The boy swallowed hard. "Yeah, I guess I did. It is cool to see the basketball team's sponsor on a dating Web site, you know."

"Not to me," Ben answered grimly. "Now here's what I'd like you to do. Talk to your friends. Find out who was behind this and come and tell me. Can I trust you to do that?"

A whistle blew. The bandleader waved Tate to

come back. Visibly relieved, the kid nodded vigorously. "Sure."

Ben watched him lope across the field. Hopefully, the kid would soon come back with the name Ben wanted, but he wasn't going to gamble on it. He'd have to try again later.

Until then, there was a more important item on his to-do list.

First there would be a visit to his uncle. Although walking out on his own wedding hadn't been his idea to start with, he still felt he'd let his uncle down. And, in some unfathomable way, himself.

Melinda wasn't going to be an easy woman to convince to listen to him, but he was determined to try. Not for anyone else's sake, but their own. He had to convince her that, although it had been left unsaid by each of them, what was between them was real. Complicated as hell, but real.

How could he have not realized how much he cared for her?

Chapter Eleven

"Got a minute, Uncle Joseph?"

Ben's uncle regarded him silently for a moment, then held open the door. "I've been waiting for you, my boy."

Ben felt like a schoolboy again visiting the school dean. For a thirty-one-year old man, the feeling didn't sit too well. "Yeah, well, you know how it is," he remarked offhandedly. "Some things take a little more time to get around to than others. I hope I'm not too late."

"Not at all." His uncle threw an arm around Ben's shoulder and led him into the den. "I've recently experienced the same problem. Happily, it looks as if I'm not too late."

"With Ms. Bertie?"

His uncle stopped to look at him. His lips twitched in a smile above his silver-streaked goatee. "How did you know?"

"By the way the two of you looked at each other at the wedding."

"I suppose there's nothing more transparent than

an old fool in love,'' his uncle laughed. He went over
to the small bar that filled a corner of the den. ''I was
just about to pour myself a bit of your remarkable
brandy. Join me?''

''Nothing, thanks. I've got to keep my head on
straight or I'll never get through this.'' Ben dropped
into an upholstered armchair, sat back and regarded
his uncle. ''You're not that old and you're not a fool,
Uncle Joseph. Not if you have the good sense to care
for a great lady like Ms. Bertie.''

''Indeed.'' His uncle carried his drink to the armchair facing Ben's and took a sip. ''I do care a great
deal for Tildy.''

''Tildy?''

Amused, his uncle explained. ''I gave Bertie that
name long ago. Bertilda seemed too somber a name
for a romantic young girl.''

It was Ben's turn to smile. ''You could say the lady
is still romantic.''

They traded grins. ''I take it you approve?''

''Why not? I know how much you loved aunt Martha, but she's been gone for several years. We both
miss her, but there's no reason for you to live alone.''

His uncle studied him in a way that made Ben
squirm. He remembered that expression too well.
''And you, Benjamin? You're a lot younger than I
am. There's no reason for you to live alone, either, is
there?''

Ben shrugged. ''I thought I wasn't the marrying
kind. I guess I proved it to myself the other day.''

''I understand you bolted from your wedding for
Melinda's sake. Very noble, but unnecessary,'' his

uncle added dryly. He took another sip of brandy and nodded his approval. "You loved the stories I used to tell you when you were young. If you have time, I'd like to tell you another one now."

Ben settled back in his chair and regarded his uncle with a whimsical smile. "Something tells me this story isn't going to be the usual parable, Uncle Joseph. Maybe a real one. Right?"

"Right." His uncle drained his glass and placed it on the coffee table. "It concerns a young and foolish man who didn't take the time to realize how much he cared for a young woman he met while home on holiday. She was bright, lovely to look at and fun to be with. So much so, the young man forgot to tell her how much he *did* care for her. Instead, he went off to finish his schooling. They never met again until recently."

"She didn't happen to bake great chocolate-chip cookies, did she?"

His uncle smiled. "I think he remembered to tell her so before he left," he said wryly. "At any rate, upon graduation, the young man met a young woman—the daughter of a friend of the family. He fell in love, married and cherished her until the day came when he lost her several years ago."

"Aunt Martha," Ben murmured.

His uncle threw him a quelling glance. "I'm the one telling this story, my boy."

When Ben looked properly contrite, his uncle went on. "In time, they returned to his hometown so he could claim his inheritance. They were happy together, but unfortunately they had no children of their own. So they adopted his orphaned nephew, and he became the son of their hearts. All went well and in time, the boy grew up to be a man to be proud of.''

''Uncle Joseph,'' Ben protested. ''I hope you're not saying that you're not proud of me now!''

''I'm not finished with the story. Why don't you wait and see what you can make of it.''

Ben sat back.

''This same boy gave his heart away while he was in college, only to have it broken a year later by a divorce. Maybe he was too young to be a husband,'' his uncle shrugged, ''but somehow he decided there had to be something wrong with him. He decided he was never going marry again. Maybe he became afraid to give his heart away for fear it would be broken again.

''Unfortunately,'' Ben's uncle went on, as Ben remained silent, ''that meant there would be no one to carry on his family name or pass on his inheritance to. Or a woman out of his past to lighten his life.'' Ben's uncle waved Ben off when he started to protest. ''Forget the material things—in the long run they don't matter. What really counted was that, if he didn't change, he would never know the love of a bright and lovely woman and possibly children to fill his heart with joy.''

Ben finally understood why his uncle's eyes lit up whenever he mentioned Bertie. She was the woman his uncle had passed up years ago. Fate had sent him his Martha, but it was obvious his uncle had kept the memory of his first love in his heart all these years.

As for having children to carry on the Howard name, Ben was it.

Ben sat back and closed his eyes. The mental picture of Melinda in her bridal dress rose in front of him. The memory of the anguish in her eyes when she'd said she couldn't marry him twisted his heart-strings all over again.

What a fool he'd been not to have told Melinda he cared for her the first moment he'd realized it. And, to his surprise, that he was falling in love with her.

Ben's suspicion that his uncle and Melinda's aunt had played a part in Ben's photograph on the Internet faded away. That they could have been in collusion to bring him and Melinda together was possible—but considering his uncle's integrity and Bertie's belief in destiny, it became highly improbable. Besides, according to his uncle, he'd connected with Bertie again only after he'd seen Melinda's pending marriage announcement. He'd been a fool to even think anything else.

"That's some story, Uncle Joseph. I'm glad you and Ms. Bertie found each other," Ben said sincerely. "I'm afraid I haven't been that lucky."

"On the contrary, my boy," his uncle countered. "You've been very lucky. You have only to open your heart. It's long past time for you to put your unhappy experience with marriage behind you. You have a second chance at happiness in Melinda. Don't blow it."

Ben wished he could agree, but he wasn't convinced he had a chance. He raked his fingers through his hair and rubbed the back of his neck in his frustration. "She doesn't want any part of me."

"Only your heart," his uncle corrected. "And only if you're ready to give it freely. Melinda deserves the best."

Ben stood to leave. His uncle was right. He would never gain his heart's desire by living in the past or mooning over what might have been. "I'm going to try. In fact, I came here to tell you so. And to tell you that it's not because of an inheritance, or to carry on the Howard name. I've discovered I want Melinda for herself, and not for any of the baggage that comes with her."

His uncle raised his glass in a salute. "Go for it, Benjamin! You have my blessing."

BEN WAITED TWO DAYS for Melinda to reclaim her luggage. Then he caved in and brought it to her. When she opened the door, she was wearing the same sleeveless white cotton shirt that exposed the exquisite swell of her breasts and tantalizing pink flesh. The denim shorts left her shapely, golden legs exposed. Unfortunately, she had worry lines on her forehead.

He thought she was every bit as beautiful in her casual clothing as she had been in her wedding finery. And, heaven help his good intentions, a lot more sexy.

Her lips parted; a wariness flickered in her eyes. Before she could speak, he hefted her suitcases into the entry. "I brought back your luggage."

"Thank you." It wasn't her gratitude that drew his attention. It was the troubled look in her eyes.

He was tempted to reach down and smooth out the

wrinkles on her forehead with his lips. And kiss that unhappy look from her eyes. Maybe later.

"To tell the truth," he confessed with an embarrassed smile, "I intended to keep the luggage at my place until you showed up to claim it. I figured it was a sure way to give me a chance to see you again. Unfortunately you outwaited me."

"That's because there's nothing to talk over. At one time or another, I think we said it all." She reached for her overnight bag.

"I don't think so," he said quietly, with a staying hand on her wrist. "I think there was a lot left unsaid, at least on my part." He glanced around the empty showrooms that opened from the small entryway. "Is there anyone else at home?"

She pulled her hand away from his. Her eyes narrowed. "Why?"

"I'd rather have you all to myself. I have something to tell you."

For a moment he thought she was going to ask him to leave. A spark of hope ran through him when she answered. "If you're worried about your uncle, he and Aunt Bertie said something about looking up a favorite place of theirs."

It was obvious from the way she looked at him that she didn't want him here, but he didn't care. After his talk with his uncle, he had so many thoughts spilling over themselves he couldn't wait to share them with her.

That small voice in the back of his mind told him Melinda was just as unhappy about their circumstances as he was. And that, if she was still upset with him, she would have sent him on his way by now.

"May I come inside?" He held his breath, hoping the small voice whispering in his head was right.

The worry lines on her forehead grew deeper. She stared at him for a long moment. "Will you promise to leave when I ask you to?"

He smiled his agreement. He couldn't have walked away even if he'd wanted to. Not when the unhappy look in her eyes struck such a responsive chord in him.

He wanted to take her in his arms and assure her he was going to make everything right for her—for them. The shock that he might lose her had awakened him to the truth; she'd been right on target about their relationship. He hadn't really cared for her at the time. Not the way she'd wanted him to.

Gazing into green eyes clouded by changing emotions, he wondered how he could have fallen in love with Melinda and not realized it. Everything about her was memorable. Even her faint, sweet honeysuckle scent was driving him crazy.

Now was as good a time to clear things up. "Had your morning coffee yet?"

She looked surprised and glanced into the kitchen. "No. I put it on to perk a few minutes ago."

"Mind if I join you?" He held his breath. If she let him in, he was halfway home.

"Okay." She gave him a warning look and led the way to the kitchen. He started to follow her, then paused. Maybe it was his imagination, but the same showcase bridal mannequin that kept watch over the entry to the wedding dress showroom cast a warning glance at him as he passed.

Melinda had two cups of coffee poured by the time he'd reached the kitchen. "Cookies? Aunt Bertie baked up a storm. Says sugar solves every problem. What do you think?"

"Absolutely," he agreed, aware that she was determined to treat his visit lightly. And not let him get too close. "Not for breakfast, though. Thanks. I'll grab a few on my way out. But I'll be honest with you, I am starved. With Manuel away for vacation..."

"You don't look starved to me." She eyed him under lifted eyebrows.

"That depends on how you define starvation." He was trying to be flip. Inside his chest his heartbeat was waltzing to three-quarter time.

The ironic look she turned on him would have downed a less determined man. The way he saw it, she was clearly debating what she should safely offer him before he wore out his welcome.

"I was about to make breakfast for myself. I guess I could make something for you."

Ben breathed an inward sigh of relief. If Melinda was inviting him to stay for breakfast, maybe things weren't as bad as he thought. Otherwise, it would have been coffee and out.

While the aroma of sizzling bacon mingled with the lingering smell of chocolate, he checked out the kitchen. It wasn't the first time he'd felt the kitchen was inviting. But he'd never been so aware of the woman in it.

Everything about Melinda was inviting, he thought

idly as he studied her. She was born to be some man's devoted companion, wife and mother of his children. Too bad some decent guy hadn't noticed her qualities by now. On the other hand, maybe fate *was* playing into his hands. Maybe it wasn't too late for him.

He watched while she scrambled eggs and deftly dropped slices of bread into a waiting toaster. His mouth was watering by the time she buttered the toast and put it on a small plate. She turned and, noticing his eyes on her, dropped the toast. When she knelt to pick it up, he bent to help her. Their hands touched. Their eyes met. There was a question in her eyes, an answer in his. Their lips almost touched. If she hadn't jumped to her feet and moved out of his way, he would have kissed her.

Her fingers grazed his again when she handed him his plate. Her touch made him want to pull her into his lap and show her just how hungry he was. She might not want him, but he damn well wanted her. And not only to touch. He wanted to share his discovery that he loved her. And to show her how much. He took a deep swallow of hot coffee and muttered his distress. Now he was burning inside and out.

He ate silently for a few moments before she pushed away her untouched plate. "You wanted to talk?"

He'd spent the last two days rehearsing a speech intended to convince her he was a changed man, but there was still a hollow ache in his stomach that no food would ever fill.

He drained his coffee cup and sat back. "Just this.

I need to tell you all the things I should have told you days ago before the wedding.''

"Wedding?'' She smiled bitterly and started to clear the table. "You mean the farce we planned with your friend Dex as the minister.''

"Maybe, maybe not,'' he answered as he rose to help. "I was a prize jerk for coming up with that stupid fake-minister idea. But things are different now. Just listen to me for a few minutes. Okay?''

His heartbeat went back to normal when she nodded, refilled their coffee cups and sat down. "It wasn't until yesterday that I finally realized I haven't been honest with myself...or with you.'' Her eyebrows rose. He forged ahead.

"It occurred to me I've been a fool. The truth is, my divorce hurt more than I was willing to admit. Since then, I've been afraid to let a woman, any woman, get too close. Or to commit myself to a relationship.''

Her face grew still. A glimmer of compassion showed in her eyes, but her lips remained grim.

He went on while he still had the chance. "Your refusing to go through with your wedding fantasy was a wake-up call. In fact, I've found out more about myself in the last few days than I have for years. I've been a prize idiot. I should have told you how much I'd grown to care for you. I was afraid you'd only laugh at me, so I used my uncle's ultimatum as an excuse to charge ahead with the wedding plans.''

He took a deep breath and went on. "I've spoken to my uncle and admitted what a fool I've been. And then I came here.''

"And what did your uncle have to say?"

"He told me the story about him and your aunt and how lucky he is for them to have found each other again. Before he was through, I realized their story could be ours. Only I don't want to wait thirty-five years before I tell you how much I've grown to care for you."

He watched conflicting emotions cross Melinda's face. Confessing he'd been stupid wasn't easy, but Melinda was no ordinary woman. He had to take a chance on her. "So, how about trying again?"

Obviously torn, she shook her head. "A marriage of convenience isn't enough for me," she answered. "I want more."

"It wouldn't be a marriage of convenience," he protested. "I'm talking about a real marriage with a real minister and a real honeymoon. We could even cash in on your honeymoon award. I thought I was making that clear. If I haven't..."

"I'm sorry." Melinda shook her head again. "I would be compromising everything I believed in if I said yes. Even a real marriage between us wouldn't be enough."

He ached to take her in his arms and convince her their time had come. "What *would* be enough?"

She carried their empty cups to the sink. When she turned back, the look on her face told him his luck had run out.

"I couldn't marry a man who believes I'm not truthful."

He felt as if the biblical Walls of Jericho had tumbled down on him.

"Physical attraction isn't enough," she went on. "Not even love is enough. Without trust, there can't be a real marriage."

"You're talking about my accusing you of putting my photograph on the dating Web site, aren't you?" She nodded.

He searched his mind to find something to say to convince her he'd changed. He came up empty, but he'd come too far to turn back. "What if I told you I believe you now?"

"Why now and not before?"

"I guess I shot from the hip," Ben answered with an ironic smile. "If I've learned anything about you, Melinda, it's that you're as honest as they come. And that you're too loving and caring a woman to intentionally hurt anyone. By itself, that fantasy of yours was harmless. I should have let it go. We could have passed it off as a joke. We couldn't have been a larger topic of conversation than we are now."

"I was the one who pressed the enter key." she said honestly. "In a way, I'm as guilty as you are."

"Maybe," he agreed. "But you reconsidered as soon as you realized what I was planning was wrong—that the whole idea was wrong. *I* was the one who insisted we go through with the charade with Dex. But that's in the past. It's the future I'm talking about. I came to tell you I care a lot about you. And that I'd like us to try again."

The house was eerily silent as he waited for her answer. He had to have that answer now, before his uncle and Bertie came home. "Melinda?"

"I'm sorry, it's still too late." She dried her hands

with a towel and came back to the table. "Who knows what else I might say or do later on that you might not believe? I can't live like that. When I do marry, the marriage will be for real. And to a man who not only cares for me, he trusts me."

Frustrated, Ben shot back. "Like I said before, you don't want a man, you want a saint." He knew himself well enough to know he was no saint, nor would he probably ever be. But he wanted Melinda enough to try to compromise. "I can't promise you perfection, but I'm willing to try. I made a promise to help you and I intend to keep it." His heart was thundering inside.

"Perhaps you're right," Melinda answered after a long moment of silence. "Since I'm no saint, I don't have the right to expect you to be one, either." She gazed at him candidly. "I'm afraid I'm going to need some time for me to get used to the idea."

Saint or no, Ben grimly realized, the time when he could hold her in his arms and make her his was going to be soon.

"I'd better get on the sainthood project right away," he announced. "I'll be back. But before I go, I want to go on record. What is between us isn't over. I don't intend to give up on you."

He liked the way her eyes lit up, the worry lines faded. He plunged on. "Just to prove how serious I am about helping you change your mind, I'm going to try to put the bridal shop on its feet. So when it is, you won't have to think about marrying anyone for your aunt's sake." He bent forward and fixed her with his sincerity. "You won't have to think about anything but how much I care for you."

Melinda's mind whirled with questions. Aside from the decision to actually marry Ben, there *was* the bridal shop to consider. "How can you put the shop on its feet? I've tried everything I could think of to turn it around. I've cut the cost of weddings to the bone. I've offered wedding gowns at discount prices in the local newspaper. Not even the bridal referral service I started has helped."

"Simple. I'll use the same advertising approach I used to put my Oak Tree brandy on its feet. By letting the world know you're here. If that doesn't work, I'll try to come up with something else until it does," he went on doggedly.

"I don't have that kind of money!"

"You don't need money. All you need to know is how to use the Internet." He eyed her humorously. "I gather you're pretty good at that."

She nodded reluctantly, but she couldn't keep a smile from hovering at the corner of her lips.

"So, when the time comes for me to ask you to marry me for real, your answer will be for your own sake, not for Aunt Bertie or anyone else. Besides," he added, "now that my uncle is in the picture, I don't think she has a problem. I'm willing to bet the two of them get together in the next few months. Maybe even sooner."

Instead of being relieved, Melinda felt more frustrated than ever. "Aunt Bertie is too proud to take anything from your uncle—if they do marry. And so am I! You may not give up easily, but neither do I.

I'm sure I can come up with something new sooner or later without your help!''

Ben shrugged, but his smile was knowing. "Face it, Melinda, your aunt is in love. When people are in love, nothing else matters. Not even a bridal shop."

"It matters to me!"

A calculating look came into his eyes. "We'll have to wait and see if we're both human, won't we?" Before she could move, he put his hands on her shoulders and kissed her lips, once, tenderly. The second time, passionately. "Hold those for me, sweetheart. I'll be back to pick them up as soon as I put a few ideas into play."

Melinda ached to ask Ben to stay. She told herself it wasn't just a matter of biology that made her want him—the same accusation she'd foolishly thrown at him weeks ago. An accusation she'd come to regret. The afternoon of the picnic could have been a journey into her heart's desire. Instead, it had been a stop on a fantasy that had left her alone and lonely on what should have been her wedding day.

As she stood watching Ben stride out the door, she realized her response to him was more than simple, uncomplicated biology. She may have had a crush on a boy in high school, but she'd fallen in love with the man he'd grown up to be.

Why did love have to hurt? she wondered sadly.

How many times could she bear to say goodbye?

She waited until Ben disappeared from sight before she went to a window, pulled back a lace curtain and watched him get into his open convertible. The wind blew a lock of hair into his eyes when he pulled away.

To her dismay, he looked up at the window, grinned and waved goodbye before he pulled away. Was there nothing the man missed?

She let the curtain fall back into place, but Ben's smile lingered. He was strong, ruggedly handsome and self-assured. If he said he would think of something to put the bridal shop back on its feet, she had no doubt that he would be able to do it. She didn't doubt he'd come back to collect his kisses, either. Heat raced down her spine when she touched her fingers to her lips.

His uncle had said Ben was a man who knew what he wanted and settled for nothing less than the stars. She'd never thought of herself as a star, or beautiful, either. If Ben thought so, maybe it was because there was an old saying that a woman *was* beautiful to a man who loved her.

Ben Howard was everything she wanted in a man—if only she could believe she was everything he wanted in a woman.

Chapter Twelve

Drat the man! She'd spent the last hour wondering when Ben would come back to collect his kisses.

Melinda put aside her thoughts of Ben and decided to stop feeling sorry for herself. Today was the Fourth of July, her birthday and her favorite holiday. She wasn't going to let anyone or anything ruin it for her. Certainly not Ben.

She lay back against her pillows and let her mind wander back through the years when she was eight and had come to live with her aunt. Bertie had tried to comfort her by telling her the entire country was helping celebrate her birthday. After all, she'd been lovingly told, she had no right to be sad since she was luckier than most children. Which of her friends had such exciting fireworks displays on their birthdays?

She hopped out of bed, threw open her windows and breathed in the gardenia-scented air that wafted in from the park across the street. The larger-than-planned gardenia bushes that had been planted for her wedding had turned out to have been Zoe's doing. With a little persuasion from Ben's uncle Joseph, the nursery had decided to donate the bushes to the city as a tax write-off.

It was the numerous other bills that had her worried.

One was the larger-than-expected caterer's bill that had arrived yesterday. Bertie had told her not to worry, but how could she not worry?

Melinda was afraid to contemplate how her aunt intended to pay them. Unless the company planned on including chocolate-chip cookies in their menus. Baking would keep her aunt busy for weeks.

Thankfully, most of the smaller bills had been paid off with her aunt's or Zoe's barter system.

She put her thoughts behind her and smiled with pleasure at the preparations for the community picnic at the park. And for the fireworks display that would follow at sundown.

The gazebo where she'd once dreamed of being married had been stripped of its floral decorations. Decorated in red-white-and-blue flags, it had been turned into a bandstand. Flags were flying throughout the park. Even the migratory birds were singing in the trees.

It was a lovely day for a birthday.

Just as she turned away to shower and dress, a movement in front of the house caught her eye. She took a closer look. Two high school boys were handing out colorful flyers to passing pedestrians. That wasn't unusual. What was unusual was the way pedestrians were turning to gaze at the bridal shop after they glanced at the flyer. Something definitely was up.

She showered and dressed in her new sundress and hurried downstairs. The doorbell sounded.

"Can you get that, dear?" Her aunt's voice came from the kitchen, along with the scent of cookies baking.

Melinda checked her wristwatch. It was barely nine o'clock, hardly time for clients. Unless...

She swung open the door. The caller thrust a yellow flyer under her nose. "Hi! I came to collect."

"Collect?" Melinda studied the young ponytailed woman dressed in a denim jumper, rubber sandals and little else. Braces were on her teeth. "Collect what?"

Brown eyes clouded. She waved the flyer again. "Isn't this yours?"

"Pardon me?" Melinda said with a studied smile as she reached for the paper. "Do you mind waiting until I read what it says?"

"Sure, go ahead," the young woman replied, popping her bubble gum. "I thought I'd better take the tour before the crowds show up. And the cookie, too," she added with a disarming grin.

Cookie? Tour? Crowds? Melinda hurriedly scanned the yellow advertisement that was covered with giant, bold flyer letters. To her dismay, it offered a tour of Bertie's Bridal Shop. That wasn't all. One of Bertie's famous chocolate-chip cookies was included at the end of the tour to anyone who presented the flyer within the next twenty-four hours.

Melinda didn't know anything about the offer, but she was beginning to have a pretty good idea who was behind it. The sound of cookie tins rattling in the kitchen and the scent of chocolate were a dead give-away.

"Sure, go on ahead. I'll join you in a minute."

Melinda headed for the kitchen and waved the flyer. "Aunt Bertie, do you know anything about this?"

"Why, yes, dear." Her aunt glanced up from the tray of cookies she was setting out to cool. "It's what they call a promotion. To bring prospective brides into the shop."

"Who's 'they,' Aunt Bertie?" Melinda asked. Had her aunt found a soul mate?

"Why, your Benjamin, of course. He had the flyers printed up for me and hired some young men to pass them out. Joseph is proud of him. And so am I."

"Aunt Bertie," Melinda said ominously, "he's not my Benjamin. Not that it's a bad idea, but don't you think it would have been better if the offer had been confined to women of marriageable age? The girl who just came to collect can't be more than sixteen, if that."

Her aunt stopped to consider. A frown creased her forehead before she brightened. "Maybe she has an older sister!"

Melinda closed her eyes and said a silent prayer for patience. Aware that her aunt had made it this far by looking at life as a half-filled glass, she didn't have the heart to pursue the issue. But, even if Joseph approved of his nephew's idea, Ben was moving too fast. She turned to go back to her caller.

The doorbell rang again. Melinda cast a wary eye

on the ponytailed girl who was gazing into a display case. She would have to wait.

"Good morning!" the new caller said brightly. "We came to collect on your offer."

Melinda glanced over the caller's shoulder. Three more young women stood behind her regarding her expectantly. And not one of them was older than sixteen.

She held open the door. "Sure, come on in." Each of the four new visitors handed her a flyer as they wandered into the hall. "Cool!" their leader commented as she gazed enviously at the bridal mannequin. "I just love looking at wedding dresses, don't you?"

Melinda had had enough. Buying instead of looking at bridal dresses would have been more like it. One thing was clear. If she didn't put a stop to the flyer caper, the house would be full of teenage girls eating chocolate-chip cookies and drooling over bridal dresses. The chances of any of them having an older sister who was in the market for a wedding dress was slim to none.

"Do you mind telling me where you got these?"

"Over at band practice," one of the girls said over her shoulder as she wandered to the adjoining room where the bridal shop's inventory of wedding dresses were hung in clear plastic garment bags.

"Tell you what," Melinda offered when it was clear she was stuck with the girls. She stopped long enough to attract the attention of her first visitor. "Why don't you all go into the kitchen and collect your chocolate-chip cookies from Ms. Bertie. When we have a few more visitors, I'll take all of you on a tour. In the meantime, I have a call to make.''

Melinda's suggestion was met with a chorus of giggles. She watched them troop through the doorway into the kitchen. Her conscience at sending them there was clear. Bertie would be delighted to have an audience. She would happily entertain the lot of them until the supply of cookies ran out. And, if she knew her aunt, they would all soon be baking up a storm.

A hurried check of the telephone book gave her the telephone number of Ben's distillery.

''Ben Howard here!''

''It's a good thing, too!'' Melinda burst out. ''What possessed you? How could you work up an advertisement offering a tour of the bridal shop without consulting me? Let alone offer a chocolate-chip cookie to just anyone who was interested?''

''Why not? I thought it was a great idea. The flyers are on me. All it'll cost your aunt is the cost of a cookie.''

She tried to reign in her temper. ''And the purpose behind the offer?''

''To sell wedding gowns, of course. I thought that that was what you wanted?''

''To children?'' She couldn't help keep the facetious tone out of her voice.

''Who said anything about children?'' Ben's puzzled voice grew wary. ''Kids don't need wedding dresses…do they?''

''Maybe for Halloween,'' Melinda allowed. ''Too bad the flyer didn't say adults only. The least you could have done was to add a qualifying minimum age to the offer!''

"Yeah, well, we'll do that next time. Sorry."

Melinda tried to keep her cool, but it was obvious to her Ben was trying hard to keep from laughing. He might think the whole thing was funny, but she didn't!

"On the other hand," he added before she could tell him what she thought of him and his merchandising schemes, "maybe they have an older sister who's thinking of getting married? Or maybe there's a single mother who's thinking of getting remarried?"

"You wish," Melinda retorted. "You should have been aware that if you give a high school boy business flyers to hand out, he'll head for the nearest gaggle of teenage girls!"

Ben finally gave way to laughter. "You've got a point."

Melinda didn't know whether to cry or laugh with him. She let her temper fly. "Now see here, Ben Howard. If you have anymore schemes to help Aunt Bertie, you'd better try them on me first. Selling brandy isn't in the same league as selling wedding gowns. We need to have women sober enough to remember their wedding day! And in one of my aunt's wedding gowns!"

"You shouldn't complain—the ad brought *some* results, didn't it?"

She caught her breath. She wasn't getting anywhere being angry. Nor was she going to let a stupid argument over chocolate-chip cookies get in the way of Ben's promise to help put the bridal shop in the black.

When and if she took him on again, it was going to be over something more important.

"Yes, well, for your information the house is full of giggling teenagers," she told him. "I'll give them a tour of the shop, but I'd appreciate it if you went over to where the high school band is practicing and collect any of the flyers that haven't been distributed."

"Okay, but only for you, Melinda," he added in a low, sensuous voice that sent her hormones fluttering. "I'll be seeing you soon."

Melinda sat staring at the telephone. Ben's "I'll be seeing you" hung in the air long after he'd hung up and a recorded voice was saying "Please hang up and try your call again."

Ben had promised to set the bridal shop on its feet before he came back into her life, but the tour and cookie promotion was obviously a bust. She was afraid to contemplate what his next promotional stunt was going to be.

BEN DROVE OVER to the parade staging ground where the high school band and patriotic floats were gathering. The parade was scheduled to start in an hour. He didn't have high hopes of finding any remaining flyers advertising the bridal shop, but he had another fish to fry anyway. He'd been thinking about that damn picture on the Web site, and he was going to stop it once and for all.

He parked his car on the edge of the staging ground so he could approach unobserved. Band players were milling around warming up. Floats were getting their last-minute touches. In the distance, he noticed Tate huddled in earnest conversation with several of his fellow band players. Since they were all members of the basketball team he sponsored, he figured they owed him.

He quietly strolled up behind them. "What's up, fellows?"

Tate jumped. His face was flushed, his eyes sparkled. As far as Ben was concerned, the heated look on the kid's face wasn't about the parade. The topic had to be more of the female variety. Or maybe, Ben's picture on the Internet.

"Er, hi, Mr. Howard!" the kid stammered. His friends exchanged wary glances. A guilty sign if Ben had ever seen one.

"Hi, yourself," he replied. He stuck his clenched fists into his pockets. No use scaring the life out of the kids. Not when he wanted to get to the bottom of the dating Web site caper. "Thought you owed me a visit?"

"Yes, sir, I guess I did...do...that is..." Tate looked at the other boys for help. They looked as uncomfortable as he did, but not one of them uttered a sound.

"Look, fellows," Ben began when he realized he wasn't going to get anywhere with jump-starting the action. "A joke is a joke. But this Web site bit has gone beyond that." He waited while his comment sank in. "Someone has to face up to putting my photograph on the Internet. If it wasn't one of you, I expect you to tell me who did. And, if it wasn't your idea in the first place, tell me who put you up to it."

The boys looked at each other. Ben was tempted to tell them confession was good for the soul, but he didn't think teenage boys were concerned about their souls—at least not yet. High school was the time for innocence. The last thing he wanted to do was to take it away from them.

"So, how about it? Someone going to talk?"

The boys traded glances. Two of them shrugged. The other two rolled their eyes. Ben relaxed. He was making some kind of progress.

"What are you going to do to us if we did know, Mr. Howard?"

"Not a thing," Ben replied. He decided to trade on the fact that his high school reputation as a star athlete and his current sponsorship of the basketball team would make a difference. "This is a man-to-man conversation. Agreed?"

They nodded in unison. He went on. "The point is, I'm not for hire. Not for a date, or for anything else. I want to make sure my photograph gets taken off the Web site before there's any more misunderstandings. That's all. I promise. So, who was it?"

The boys looked at each other again. A silent message flowed between them before the saxophone player, Brett Thompson, took a deep breath. "I guess it was me."

"You *guess?*"

"Yeah, well, it was me. I'm the only one of us who knows how to infiltrate a Web site." He took a step backward at the grim look that came over Ben's face. "It was only a joke, honest. I'll take it off right away."

"There was nothing honest about it," Ben said disgustedly. "Any other Web sites involved?"

"No, that is…no," Brett stammered.

"You mean not yet?"

"No, sir. Not yet." The kid gulped.

"Maybe never?" Ben prompted in the hopes he'd gotten to the kid before he did any more damage. "In case you don't know, hacking is a federal offense. Unless you want to spend your senior year in juvenile court, I suggest you forget everything you know about hacking."

"Yes, sir!"

"Now that that's settled," Ben went on, relieved Ritchie hadn't been the clown with the bright idea. "Who put you up to doing it?"

"No one, I swear." Brett thrust his saxophone under one arm and thrust his right hand in the air. "We just thought it would be fun to find out what would happen if you did get some calls. We didn't expect you to get married to a woman who chose you! That is—" he glanced at Tate and heaved a sigh of relief "—almost get married. So I guess it didn't count."

Relieved to find that Melinda or Ritchie hadn't been involved after all, Ben dismissed the reference to his disastrous wedding. He treated the culprit to a look that the kid would long remember. "So, now you know I know. You're going to take my picture off the Web site and you're going to forget hacking. Right?"

Brett nodded vigorously.

"Good." Ben regarded the other boys. "That goes for the rest of you, too." He waited until they all agreed. "Okay, go on back and get ready for the parade. I'm willing to forget the whole thing, but only this once. If I hear of any of you doing something like this again…" He left the threat unsaid.

The boys tumbled over themselves getting back to the rest of the band. Ben took off shaking his head.

He knew why he'd suspected Ritchie could be the culprit—it had been the guy's misguided sense of humor. But Melinda? She might know her way around the Internet, but there wasn't a sweeter or more thoughtful person in Ojai. Maybe Bertie. Stupid!

Overhead, a Goodyear blimp was gliding toward the center of Ojai. A mammoth sign was floating from its side: Happy Fourth Of July Courtesy Of Bertie's Bridal Shop. On the other side, still unseen from the highway but fresh in Ben's mind, was another huge sign.

Ben smiled his satisfaction. Somewhere in the crowd that gathered for the town's annual parade, there had to be a prospective bride or two. Now maybe he would redeem himself to Melinda.

On the other hand, Ben mulled as he drove home, Brett's manipulation of the Internet gave him an idea. What if Ms Bertie's Bridal Shop was advertised on the Internet? There was no reason she had to rely solely on local trade. Given the right message, and the right type of merchandizing, wedding gowns and all the stuff that went with it could be advertised around the country. To the entire world, for that matter.

The more he thought of it, the more he was proud of himself.

Visions of orders for wedding gowns floating through cyberspace sounded right. Shopping on the Internet was the latest craze. Why couldn't Bertie take advantage of the newest trend in merchandizing? In no time, she could get rid of the large inventory of wedding gowns she probably had signed up for with the Happy-Ever-After Bridal Gown Company. According to Melinda, there had been no other way for her to win a honeymoon.

Just the thought of spending a week with Melinda in a railway compartment sent his testosterone surging.

As far as the rail honeymoon went, unfortunately it would have to keep. First he had to build up Bertie's Bridal Shop and then persuade Melinda to marry him again.

One thought led to another. The longer he thought of it, his plans grew as grandiose as the blimp that was following him down the highway.

But first things first. Melinda's aunt had remarked to his uncle that today was Melinda's birthday. His uncle hadn't wasted any time in passing the information on to Ben. Ben grinned and glanced up at the blimp. Today was going to be celebrated in style.

TUCKING A WISP of hair behind her ear, Melinda dashed for the door. Dressed in immaculate whites, a waiter stood in the door. He held a large picnic basket decorated in red, white and blue streamers in one hand. In the other, he held a single, long-stemmed red rose tied with a red ribbon. "Miss Melinda Carey?"

Her mind awhirl with possibilities, Melinda tried to

remember if this had been part of her fantasy wedding creation. Impossible. She nodded cautiously.

"Happy Fourth of July," he said with a broad smile. "Oh, and happy birthday." He handed her the red rose.

"Thank you." She searched in her pocket for a tip. She hesitated. "How did you know it was my birthday?"

"The tip was included, Miss Carey." He handed her the picnic basket. "As for your birthday, I guess everyone knows it by now." He saluted and left.

Melinda eyed the picnic basket warily. How did everyone know today was her birthday? There was no card, but she was pretty sure she knew who had sent it. No one else she knew was inclined to send roses— except for her aunt Bertie's Joseph. Her aunt had often commented that the apple didn't fall far from the tree.

She held the red rose to her lips and inhaled its lovely scent. She knew red was the color of everlasting love. Ben? she wondered, as the red velvet petals glinted under the mid-afternoon sun streaming through the door.

Roses were nice, but no substitution for spending her birthday without the man she'd grown to love. He'd told her he would be back when he kept his promise. Maybe the rose and the picnic basket were reminders he hadn't forgotten. Although she was touched, her heart was empty.

"Melinda? Who was at the door? Someone with another one of those advertisements?" Her aunt came into the hall beaming. "Imagine, we've had more than fifty visitors. I've just made another batch of cookies!''

"No, a deliveryman, Aunt Bertie." Melinda stroked the rose with a tender smile.

"A deliveryman? On a holiday?'' Her aunt eyed the picnic basket. "It must have been something important.''

"You could say so," Melinda agreed dreamily, her thoughts on the sender. "Someone sent us a picnic lunch.''

"A picnic lunch? How thoughtful." Her aunt bent over the basket and looked for a card. "Who sent it, dear? Joseph?''

Melinda brushed her cheek with the red rose. "I don't think so. There wasn't a card, but the deliveryman said the basket was intended for me."

Her aunt noticed the rose. "A red rose, of course." A knowing look passed over her aunt's face. "Red is for love, so the basket must be from your Benjamin. I wonder why he didn't deliver it himself?''

"I don't know, Aunt Bertie." The longing in her voice sent the smile from her aunt's face.

"Don't worry, dear. I have a hunch you'll be hearing from that young man of yours before the day is through.''

"Not after I sent him away." Melinda remembered Ben's promise to come back when he had the bridal shop flourishing with brides. "At least not yet. I guess I'll go upstairs and change for the picnic."

"Don't be too sure, dear." her aunt replied with a secret smile. "He *is* Joseph's nephew. The Howards never forget. After listening to the way Joseph speaks about his Benjamin, I'm willing to believe your young man isn't the kind to give up easily, either."

MELINDA, BERTIE and Joseph found a shady place under a tree. The picnic basket yielded hearty roast beef sandwiches, pickles, tiny cherry tomatoes, a thermos of lemonade and a bottle of wine. Dessert was a basket of fresh strawberries and chocolate kisses. Ben's uncle was pouring a glass of wine for her aunt when Martha Ebbetts ground to a halt in front of them.

"Good afternoon, Melinda," she said brightly. "You certainly are a celebrity today."

"A celebrity?" Melinda stopped to consider. "Oh, you mean because today is my birthday."

"Of course." Martha tilted her head, her eyes glittered. "But to celebrate in such a fashion with a sign like that?"

"What sign?" Melinda glanced around the park. "I don't see any sign."

"That's because you're not looking up!"

Melinda jumped to her feet and stared up into the sky. To her surprise, the Goodyear blimp was hovering overhead. She read the message across its body.

Horrified, Melinda looked down at her aunt, then back into the sky. "Aunt Bertie, tell me you didn't contract to advertise on the blimp! It must cost a fortune!"

"Certainly not," her aunt replied. She shaded her eyes and gazed up into the sun. "Although it certainly is a good idea, even if it must be very expensive. Did you do it, Joseph?"

He shook his head. "No, although I must say it's very effective."

Murmurs and laughter arose throughout the park as heads craned to read the sign. For the second time in as many days, Melinda was the center of attraction.

"Good Lord," she moaned. "All this commotion over an advertisement we didn't even place!"

"I don't think it's the advertisement for the bridal shop everyone is looking at," Martha Ebbetts replied. She gestured skyward as the blimp made a wide turn and glided back over the park.

On the other side of the blimp were the words Happy Birthday, Melinda. Marry Me!

Speechless with embarrassment, Melinda put a hand over her eyes. So that was why everyone knew it was her birthday!

"It looks as if your young man has changed his mind. Maybe this is his way of apologizing to you for walking out on you at your wedding." She took a small pad and pencil from her purse and stood poised for Melinda's answer.

Melinda's heart raced as calls wishing her a happy birthday were coming from all over the park. A few women called to Melinda not to make it too easy on Ben before she forgave him.

Poor Ben. He may have taken the blame for calling off the wedding ceremony, but it looked as if Martha Ebbetts considered it just another episode in a daytime TV drama.

Who else would have sent a picnic basket and arranged to put a mammoth sign in the sky wishing her a happy birthday but Ben?

Who else had the innovative type of mind and the money to come up with the outlandish scheme?

She looked up again, half expecting to see red roses raining down from the sky. That's all she needed to become the subject of the front page of the newspaper.

"Mr. Howard." The society reporter turned to Joseph and went on, her pencil poised. "What is your opinion?"

"Other than to wish Melinda a very happy birthday, I have none," he replied with a wink at Melinda. "Why don't we all wait and see?"

"Wait for what?" Martha Ebbetts asked with a quick glance around her. "I have to have the answer for tomorrow's edition."

"I'm afraid you'll have to wait for Melinda to give you the answer to that question," he smiled. "And I don't think even she knows it yet."

Melinda shook her head and forced a smile. She did have to wait and see. After what he'd come up with so far, if Ben ran true to form, she hadn't seen anything yet.

Chapter Thirteen

Melinda stood riveted, her gaze on the Goodyear blimp that continued to circle the park. In the background, drums, trumpets and a cacophony of wind instruments sounded. The park began to empty as everyone rushed to the curb to watch the parade go by.

"Coming, dear?"

"No thanks, Aunt Bertie," Melinda answered. "I think I'll watch from here."

With an apologetic smile, Joseph took her aunt's hand and led her away. Martha Ebbetts threw Melinda an uncertain look and rushed after them.

Melinda had too much on her mind to even think about joining them. Today, the parade's homemade floats that normally fascinated her with their ingenuity held no attraction. It wasn't everyday a woman got a proposal courtesy of a two-thousand-pound balloon.

"Happy birthday," a voice whispered from behind her. A warm breath brushed her ear. A hand came over her shoulder and gently turned her around. A finger gently touched her lips to caution her to silence.

"Ben?"

"Who else?" Ben smiled down at her. "Before you say anything, I know I promised you I wouldn't come back until I had Ms. Bertie's shop out of the red. I also remember promising to let you call the shots in our relationship." He ran a forefinger over her lips; his eyes danced with mischief. "I couldn't help myself. I couldn't let this day go by without at least giving you a birthday kiss."

Melinda's eyes stung. She hadn't been able to get Ben out of her thoughts from the first moment she'd seen his photograph on the Internet. Maybe, she thought through a happy mist of tears, if you wished hard enough, wishes would come true. "Just having you here is enough."

"Not nearly enough," he answered, "but hearing you say you're glad to see me is a good beginning, sweetheart." He cradled her head between his hands, gently massaged the corners of her mouth with his thumbs and bent to her lips.

The parade, the music, the park and everyone in it faded away. She felt as though she were standing on a deserted island with no sound to break the silence that surrounded them other than Ben's whispered endearments.

This was the Ben she'd been dreaming about. The athletic beauty of him, the affectionate humor shinning from his eyes filled her heart with joy. He was the man her heart couldn't reject even after her mind had warned her to beware of sky-blue eyes and killer smiles.

She told herself to go slowly; he still had promises

to keep. But once he lowered his mouth to her and took her lips in hers, she was lost. She leaned against him, put her arms around his neck and kissed him back. All the longing she'd kept hidden below the surface to shield herself from being hurt surfaced. She strained to get even closer, ached to become a part of him. After days of trying to make herself believe she'd been right in calling off their wedding, she knew she'd followed her fears instead of her heart.

Ben was no saint, thank goodness, she thought dimly as she clung to him. She knew better now. He was a flesh and blood man, with all the foibles that came with the territory. She was a woman who wanted so desperately to be a part of him. Now that she was in his arms again, she never wanted to let him go.

"Ben? Can you stay a while?"

He shook his head. Then, with soft words of endearment, he kissed her deeply and nuzzled the side of her throat. She tasted of strawberries and chocolate. Her scent was of sunshine and gardenias, her kisses a promise of paradise. "I want you so very much," she whispered into his lips.

"I want you, too, sweetheart, but I have promises to keep," he answered. He kissed the tiny freckles that marched across her nose. He wasn't too happy at having to put her off. He ached to have her in his arms some place private where he could show her how much he wanted her. But not now. Making her his would have to wait.

"Which promise? The promise to help Aunt Bertie?"

"Yes," he said with an ironic grin. "I'm going to keep that promise. As for the promise to let you call the shots, I'm giving up on it." He kissed the tip of her nose. "I'm not willing to wait that long."

"You don't have to wait anymore," she whispered with a smile. "I'm ready whenever you are."

"I wish." He tenderly outlined the lips that tasted of ripe strawberries with his tongue. Their piquant taste was like Melinda herself. Sharp, then sweet and unforgettable. "You'll never know how much."

"Show me?"

He looked over her shoulder to where the parade was winding its way down Main Street and out of sight. Revelers had started to wander back to the bandstand. He sighed and shook his head.

"I'd better go now," he said reluctantly. "I see Martha pumping my uncle. The last thing we need is to wind up on page one of the newspaper."

"When will I see you again?"

"Soon." He pulled away, then turned back. "That's another promise I intend to keep. You can bet on it. Enjoy your birthday, sweetheart." He put all his longing for her into his eyes.

Melinda wanted to call him back. Although his unusual way of proposing to her had come as a shock, he *had* asked her to marry him. She'd been so taken by his presence, she'd forgotten to ask him how soon. She couldn't wait. This time around it would be a marriage of love between two people who truly cared for each other.

Martha Ebbetts started babbling as soon as she reached Melinda's side. "So, back to my question.

What do you think Ben's motive was in putting that sign on the blimp? An apology? If so, are you going to forgive him for walking out on your wedding? Are you going to marry him?''

"I'm not sure." Melinda answered, remembering Ben's kiss. She noticed a question on her aunt's face. Her romantic aunt, in love with Joseph, surely guessed Ben had been here. It was a secret she wasn't willing to share with anyone else just yet. "But I promise you, Ms. Ebbetts, you'll be the first to know when I am."

The newspaper reporter sighed her frustration. "I had hoped to put your answer in my column tomorrow. But I'll hold you to your promise. Don't forget, if you decide to accept his proposal, let me know right away."

Melinda agreed. Martha Ebbetts may not have heard the "when" instead of the "if" in Melinda's answer, but her aunt's face lit up with a brilliant smile.

BEN TOOK A spot at the end of Main Street where he could corner his target as soon as the band began to disperse.

The drummers pounded out their last hurrah. Relieved marchers dispersed; a few limped away. The musician Ben was waiting for was in the process of wiping the mouthpiece of his instrument.

Ben sauntered over to Brett Thompson. "Got a minute?"

Brett backed away. "Gee, Mr. Howard, I swear I

haven't done anything wrong! I've been marching in the parade!''

"Yeah, I know," Ben assured him. "I've got a proposition for you."

The boy eyed him warily. "What kind of proposition?"

"Nothing that will get you in trouble." Ben smiled at the kid's sigh of relief. "This is a business proposition. Strictly on the up and up."

"What do I have to do?"

"I'd like to hire you to create a Web site."

"Oh no," Brett said hastily. "I promised to stay off the Internet."

"I said create a Web site. Not hack into one."

Brett hesitated, glanced around cautiously. "What kind of a Web site?"

Ben smiled. It was an offer no red-blooded kid could refuse. Two down, and one to go.

THE BRIDAL SHOP'S telephone began to ring nonstop the next afternoon.

The first call was from a new bridal magazine confirming an ad for Bertie's Bridal Shop. In return, the caller requested the shop give a copy of the magazine to the many prospective brides who frequented the shop.

Melinda saw dollar signs. There had to be a catch. No one gave anything away for free. Even Bertie bartered for something in return. "How much will the ad cost?"

"Nothing, this is a promotion for our new magazine," her caller replied.

Without mentioning that the numbers of looky loos and chocolate-chip cookie lovers far exceeded the number of prospective brides, Melinda cautiously agreed.

She fielded calls from insurance salesmen eager to have the bridal shop refer prospective brides and their grooms to them. Real estate salesmen were avid to set up newlyweds in a new home. To top everything off, furniture stores, including Ritchie Morrison's, called. And travel agents offered honeymoons. Melinda was tickled. The bridal business pipeline was more active than usual today. Ben had to be behind this, but it was too good to be true.

The next call was from the Happy-Ever-After Bridal Attire Company requesting a firm date for the bridal fashion show.

"Fashion show?" Melinda asked warily. "What fashion show?"

"Your representative has graciously offered your premises for our annual winter bridal gown show."

Melinda held the receiver to her burning cheek. Not Bertie again! "How much is this going to cost us?"

"Why, nothing," the caller answered. "Considering the volume of orders you've placed with our company, we thought it would be good business to hold our next showing in your shop. Of course, you might like to serve some type of refreshment."

No cost? Melinda thought rapidly. "How about tea and cookies?"

"That would be fine. We'll have a contract in the mail tomorrow. Keep up the good work."

Melinda murmured her agreement and hung up.

She debated asking her aunt if she had been behind the last two calls. Until she decided that not even her aunt could have dreamed up such an incongruous scheme as a winter bridal gown show in a shop verging on bankruptcy.

What the bridal gown company might do when they finally realized they'd been had, boggled her mind. At least twelve times, she reached for the phone to call Ben. She wanted to say enough already. She wanted to stay don't stop. She wanted to say a hundred loving words and give a thousand kisses.

TWO DAYS LATER, Ben sent her an e-mail asking her if she'd watched the full moon last night. She swallowed hard. The rest of the message was businesslike. He told her to click on Bertie's Bridal Shop.com. She stared at the blue letters and viewed the incoming messages.

Melinda froze. Her aunt had a World Wide Web site? Catalogs? Her bridal referral service was being asked to plan weddings halfway across the country? No way!

Even as she watched, additional messages appeared. Some referred to cut-rate, bottom-line prices and turnaround service. She closed her eyes, aghast at the enormity of the situation. And its possibilities.

Ben!

Hadn't she told him he didn't have to keep his promise to help Bertie? Hadn't he asked her to marry him and she'd already consented to be his wife? Honor was honor, but this was ridiculous!

In the first place, she didn't have a catalog and didn't have the time nor the money to get one printed.

In the second place, she wasn't sure she could handle the volume of business by herself even if she could take advantage of the crazy situation. If she could, she mused, it just might be the way out of bankruptcy for her aunt.

She printed out the e-mail requests and considered the situation. If Ben was behind the Web site, he was going to feel the consequences. She'd add Oak Tree brandies. And, if she decided to keep the Web site and the business it generated, she'd make him a partner. It was his idea. Let him deal with the ensuing chaos.

She would have been really frustrated if the thought of Ben and co-owning a successful Web site business hadn't been so fascinating.

Of course, Bertie was dropping hints that she and Joseph were going to elope. If she did, the shop would be Melinda's to close or to nourish. Why couldn't she ask Ben to be her partner in business as well as marriage?

She came to a decision. She'd been conservative and fearful of the future long enough. If she'd learned anything from Ben, it was that it was okay to take risks. She'd also learned that there was no harm in following a dream and making it come true instead of settling for creating Internet fantasies. If she didn't, she'd never know the joy of being loved and loving in return.

She ran to her bedroom and pulled out her sexiest nightgown, the Victoria's Secret underwear she loved and had been reluctant to return. Halfway out the door, she turned back and dabbed honeysuckle perfume between her breasts and behind her ears.

"MELINDA?"

She stood there, speechless. Obviously not expecting company, Ben stood there in jeans, a shirt hastily thrown over his shoulders. His hair was damp, drops of water clung to his chin. The smell of shaving lotion clung to him.

She took a deep breath. Ignoring the uncertain smile that came over Ben's face, she high-heeled her way into the entry. She knew she came to tell him something, she just couldn't remember what.

"Melinda," he said again, a wary look on his face. He started to wipe dabs of shaving lotion from under his chin. "Is something wrong?"

"No. Something is very right," she answered. "But before I get to it, I wanted to tell you that I know you mean well, but these plans of yours have to stop! We couldn't possibly mount a bridal show or do business on the Internet, even if we had the means. You're only making a bad problem worse!"

"You'll have to trust me. We'll find a way. Besides, I'm keeping a promise," he said firmly. He drew her into the house and closed the door behind her. "Couldn't stay away, could you?"

Her mind urged caution, her heart told her to go for it. Her heart won out. For the first time in her life, she wasn't going to worry about the future. And if Ben was alone in the house...

"There's been a…glitch in my business. I thought I'd talk to you about it."

He sniffed appreciatively. "Nice perfume."

"Ben! Pay attention! I came here to talk about the Web site business you set up!"

"I am paying attention," he answered. "Just not the kind of attention you want. Or am I?" He eyed her overnight case. "The last time I ticked you off, you used the telephone." His gaze was searching, his eyes glinted with desire. An answering rush of desire filled her.

He was right. Something had brought her to Ben's house, and it wasn't to brief him on telephone solicitations. Her overnight case was a sure giveaway. She took a deep breath. "I came to release you from your promises."

"So that…?" he prompted. The look in his eyes challenged her to finish what she'd started.

She swallowed hard and took the dare. She intended to be a new woman, didn't she? In the new millennium, women didn't need to wait to be asked, did they?

"So that you could collect the kisses you left with me."

"Collect on delivery?" She nodded. The searching look he gave her told her he didn't need a second invitation. "Good enough!" He picked her up and swung her around and around until she pleaded for mercy.

"Stop! You're making me dizzy!"

"No dizzier than I am!" He carried her into the den and to the recessed conversation pit in front of the fireplace. Flowered damask-covered pillows filled the broad seats. With a deep and telling laugh, he laid her on the down pillows and dropped down beside her. "You're sure about this?"

"I'm very sure." She twisted her hands in his wavy brown hair and held him still while she made herself clear. "Let's get something straight. You asked me to marry you. Right?" He smiled. "Then my answer is yes."

He buried his lips beneath her ear and trailed kisses across her chin. "Great! When?"

Trying to get closer to him, she squirmed in his arms. "After..." She felt herself blush.

"After what?" he teased. "You're doing great. Don't stop now."

"After we make up for lost time."

He caught his breath. "It's a good thing I gave Manuel two weeks off."

Fascinated by the possibilities behind his answer, Melinda gazed at him. "Why?"

"Because I intend to make love to you in every room of the house, and it's going to take a long time." He unbuttoned her blouse, hesitating. "You're sure you want this, right?"

Speechless at the sensations running through her, she nodded. He reached behind her and stopped. "Victoria's Secret?"

She blushed. "I didn't see any point in returning them. They were meant to be used."

"And seen," he agreed. He unsnapped her bra and pressed his lips to the hollow beneath her chin.

She moaned when his lips moved to caress her

breasts. She ran her hands over his back and pressed him closer until the heat of his skin against hers matched the way he was making her feel.

"Ben, I want you so."

"Soon. Soon," he murmured, a gleam in his eyes. "Lovemaking is a game to be savored and enjoyed, sweetheart. We have today, tonight and tomorrow. And," he grinned wickedly, "after we get married, we have forever." He slid his shirt off his shoulders.

She wanted him here and now. All of him. But his eyes held promises of many more games to come. She gritted her teeth and schooled herself to play the games with him. Until her turn came. She matched him kiss for kiss, stroke for stroke. "How many rooms *do* you have?" she gasped.

"I'm not sure. We'll have to count them as we go." He slid the blouse off her shoulders. "Interesting," he said as he sat back on his heels, his hands on the button of her blue cotton pedal pushers. "You have freckles on your shoulders, too."

She didn't know if she wanted to laugh or cry with sexual frustration. She was burning with desire; he was counting her freckles! And yet, what if he intended to kiss each freckle? It might take all night! She shivered.

"If freckles are what interests you, I have a plentiful supply. In fact, I have freckles all over."

"Good enough." He paused and studied her approvingly. "I'll have to take the time to count those, too."

The magic of his hands on her middle as he reverently brushed the skin of her waist, her hips, her thighs was driving her over the edge. She couldn't take much more. She wanted to tell him it was past time for comedy and started to tell him so.

"Ben Howard, if you don't hurry up, I'm going to…" He looked up at her. Words failed her at the heated look that came into his eyes.

"You're going to do what?" The challenge in his eyes was back.

"This." She took matters into her own hands and tugged at a belt that wouldn't give. "Men," she muttered. "You have too much clothing on!"

"Let me," he said. "Things will go much faster." He stood and in a few quick movements his clothing fell to the floor.

Melinda began to realize just how in love with Ben she was. She savored Ben's bronzed shoulders, the way his muscles rippled when he undressed. His tapered waist, his unabashed manhood. "Now you." He slid her pedal pushers down her legs, tossed them next to the clothing that lay in a heap beside his. "You won't need these for a while. A long, long while."

When he dropped down beside her again, she thought she'd be embarrassed at her wanton behavior. Instead, under his admiring gaze, she was more excited than ever, anxious to move on. He was hers to love, and love him she would.

His touch, his taste, his musky scent as he came to her told her he cared for her in all the ways a man could care for a woman. Whatever had gone before faded away.

"I love you, Ben," she whispered.

"I love you, too," he answered, caressing her body with his eyes. "I'm sorry it took me so long to figure it out. But don't worry," he assured her solemnly, "I'm going to make up for lost time." He took her in his arms.

Melinda was lost. She tasted his salty skin when he slid over her. Felt the sexual friction from the rough surface of his chin when he kissed the freckles on her shoulders.

"Ben?" she moaned. "I want you so."

He slid over her and made her his. "Now, sweetheart, now."

Behind her closed eyes, giant waves rose and, like magnets, drew her under before they crashed to the shore. She was floating in warm seas, reaching for the heat of the sun that hovered above her. The storm of his lovemaking sent her spiraling upward until she touched the sun in one glorious moment. Sensation after sensation engulfed her until she couldn't think at all.

SHE SURFACED to a calmer sea, cradled in Ben's arms. One moment she'd been quietly drifting, the next, every nerve ending cried for more of him. It was more than just biology, although that was all right, too, she thought drowsily. She'd fallen in love with a man who had shown her how loving a man could be. He'd shown himself to be caring, talented, and keenly intelligent. A man who had turned apricot orchards into world-famous brandy. A man who kept his promises even when he wasn't sure of his reward.

"HI, SLEEPYHEAD," he said when he noticed she was awake. His fingers gently traced the corner of her mouth, her swollen love-kissed lips.

"I never take a nap in the daytime," she protested, jealous of the time she'd missed with him. "What happened?"

"Me?" The twinkle in his eyes was too much.

She smiled. He didn't know it yet, but he'd met his match. Now that she'd discovered two could play at the game of love, she wanted the game to go on forever. "Which room is next?"

"I was only kidding, sweetheart." He brushed her damp hair away from her sleepy eyes.

"Too bad. I'm not."

"In that case, I've had a chance to count the rooms while you were asleep," he answered thoughtfully. "There are twelve, but I'm afraid that only two of the bedrooms are furnished. That leaves those rooms out. Manuel's room, too. Of course," he went on, "there are the living room couches, the kitchen table and the billiard table in the next room." He cocked his head. "What's your pleasure?"

"You wouldn't!" Fascinated, Melinda glanced at the open door to the adjoining room. "Are you sure Manuel's gone?"

"Yes and yes." His expression was innocent, but his eyes were not. "Women aren't the only ones with fantasies. I have one or two myself." At the frustrated look she gave him, he added with the grin that had stolen her heart. "All of them include you, of course."

"Of course," Melinda echoed, not that she believed him. She wasn't going to deny him his fantasies as long as he used them on her. "I'm not too sure about the kitchen table," she said pensively. "I'd never be able to look at it without picturing what we did there. The living room couch would be okay, but..." She paused and sent him a measured look. "The billiard table sounds as if it would be more fun."

He burst out laughing and hugged her until she was sure her ribs would break. "No way. I'd never be able to play pool with a straight face again. All I'd be able to see was you lying there against the green felt backdrop and me about to join you."

She grinned. "That's bad?"

"Only if I was playing a serious game," he grinned. "So, if you haven't had enough, I have a king-size bed upstairs ready and waiting. And I'm willing," he added with a wicked leer.

She couldn't get enough of him. Where they would continue the game was fast becoming immaterial. "Think you have enough strength left to make it upstairs?"

"More than enough!"

He'd thought Melinda was shy. He'd even planned to court her in the old-fashioned way, one step at a time. Instead, she was as much a contemporary individual as he was, maybe more. She was a woman to play with, to love.

For now, he'd settle for cementing their relationship until she was ready to get married. This time for real.

He gathered her in his arms and made for the iron

staircase that wound its way to his bedroom. "And when we get there, I have a surprise for you."

He carried her into his bedroom. Instead of stopping at the king-size bed, he strode to the bathroom and through an adjacent door. "Voilà!"

He watched her eyes widen with delight. "A Jacuzzi and a steam bath! Why didn't you show it to me when I was here before?"

"I thought of it, but I didn't want you to think I was hitting on you. Game to try it now?"

She padded to the edge of the Jacuzzi and tested the water. "Not warm enough."

"It will be."

"Want to prove it?" she asked and flicked water at him.

"You have to ask?" He started for her. With a teasing look over her shoulder, she put both feet into the tub.

Making love in the Jacuzzi was something he hadn't tried, Ben mused as he watched Melinda sink into the water. With an exuberant laugh, he joined her. He was glad he'd waited for Melinda and he wasn't going to wait any longer. Now her playful, romantic mood matched his.

Hungry for more of him, Melinda floated to his side. "This is very nice," she commented lazily, "but I can't seem to keep my feet on the bottom."

He leered playfully at her. "I think you'd like it much better if your legs were curled around my waist."

Melinda considered the possibility. "You're right."

He held her while she maneuvered herself into his lap. He captured her lips, held her waist and helped her settle on his arousal.

The feel of Ben hard and strong under her sent her senses reeling. The slick sensation of heated skin sliding against heated skin with water swirling around them had to be the most erotic sensation she could have thought of. And until today, had never hoped to feel. If making love with Ben in the den had sent her into the sun, it had been only a prelude to what was happening to her now. Every nerve ending in her body tingled, heated streams of sexual fulfillment shot through her. She went beyond the sun, to the stars.

Unable to help herself, she melted against him. He tongued drops of water off her lips and kissed her deeply, passionately. "Had enough?" he murmured.

"No, never enough," she said as stars continued to shimmer over her. "I'll always want you."

"So will I," he answered. He held her in his arms until her trembling stopped. "Today, tomorrow and always."

"So," he asked when she rested in his arms worn with lovemaking, "when do you want to get married?"

"Tomorrow?"

"Get real." He laughed, tenderly wiping drops of water from her face. He kissed her damp hair. "It's going to take a least a week to plan the wedding you deserve."

"We could do the park again. It's easy to set up."

"No way," he answered, kissing the nape of her neck. "This time, I have a plan."

"Go ahead," she answered with a warning look. "As long as it's on the up-and-up with a real minister. I planned the last one. It's your turn."

"Okay. How about transforming the distillery and the surrounding grounds into an Italian villa? We'll string colored lanterns, hire a violinist or two and have dinner served dinner alfresco."

"Not with the whole of Ojai present, I hope."

He shuddered at the thought. "No. We'll only invite our friends and get married under the stars."

She leaned back. "You sound as if you've been planning this for a while."

"Well, after what happened the last time we tried to get married, I wanted some privacy. So, if you changed your mind again, it wouldn't get on the front page of the newspaper. And," he laughed, "somewhere where Ms. Zoe can't get her hands in on the planning."

"You don't have to worry, Ben." She looked up into his eyes with all the love in her. "I'll probably change my mind about a lot of things, but never about you. You can count on it."

Epilogue

A full moon shone down on the Oak Tree Distillery grounds. Transformed into an Italian villa with marble statuary and white chiffon drapes threaded through the trees, the wedding scene was everything Ben had planned, and more.

The air was scented with the sweet, pungent odor of fruit brandy and Italian delicacies. A quartet of musicians were playing Italian love songs in the background.

Ritchie peered at the musicians. "Say, the musicians are members of the high school marching band!"

Ben nodded contentedly. "Yeah. When the guys offered to play at my wedding, I decided to take them up on it. I think they're trying to make up for their sin."

"What sin was that?"

"Getting me and Melinda together through the Internet."

"That's a sin?" Ritchie regarded him warily.

"Don't tell me you want to change your mind again!"

"No way!" Ben laughed. "Rest easy."

Ritchie shifted from one foot to the other. "If I could be sure you were going through with the wedding, I'd be having a good time, too."

Ben, Ritchie at his side, gazed at the door to his office that was doubling as a dressing room for the bride. Because he'd learned a lot about sharing his deepest feelings in the last few weeks, he intended to tell her one more time how much he loved her.

As if on cue, the Reverend Charles Good, lifted his head and nodded at Ben. Ben took a deep breath.

Dressed in a short, yellow dress Joseph had admired, Bertie emerged from the tent. A single yellow rose was tucked into her bouquet of fresh spring flowers. Guests murmured their approval.

The music changed to the wedding march.

Behind her aunt, Melinda emerged wearing a confection of white silk organza. Her hair, pulled back with a wreath of white carnations, flowed around her shoulders. In the center of her bridal bouquet of matching white carnations and maidenhair fern, was a single red rose.

Amid a chorus of oohs and aahs, guests rose to their feet.

Ben's eyes locked with Melinda's. Her eyes shone with love. He sent the message back. Knowing there were many happy days ahead, he decided this was the best part of all.

When she reached him, he took her hand and held it as if he never wanted to let her go.

"Dear friends," Reverend Good began with a broad smile, "we are gathered here to join this man and this woman in holy matrimony. I've been asked, and I'm more than happy to oblige, to make my part in this ceremony brief."

To laughter, he continued. "Not because Melinda and Ben are anxious to get this ceremony over with, but because they've written their own marriage vows. I'm sure I speak for all of us when I say we are privileged to hear the words that will bind them together in God's sacrament. He beamed at Ben. "Go ahead, young man."

Ben took both of Melinda's hands in his and cleared his throat.

"My dearest Melinda. Toward the end of one of my favorite books, there's a phrase that expresses the way I feel about you. The author writes that the protagonist had waited for the perfect woman for too long. And now that he'd found her, his search was over. He made to her the same vows I make to you.

"To love you, honor you and cherish you.

"To care for you and let you care for me.

"To laugh with you and cry with you."

At this point, tears began to slide down Melinda's cheeks. Ben gently wiped the tears from the corners of her eyes before he continued.

"I promise to wipe the tears from your eyes and put smiles on your face.

"To celebrate each day that I can hold your hand, touch your face and kiss your lips.

"I will love you madly all the days of my life."

Women in the audience broke into tears. More than one man reached for his handkerchief.

"And now you, Melinda," the minister encouraged.

Melinda smiled through her tears.

"Dear Ben. I want you to know that all my dreams are coming true. You may not know it, but on the day I first saw you play in high school, I was drawn to your sparkling eyes and the joy with which you lived life on and off the basketball court.

"That initial attraction evolved into depths of admiration and affection for the wonderful man you've become.

"Your sensitivity, your uncanny intellect and the epic proportions of love and loyalty you show me, your friends and family will forever keep me captivated.

"I feel as though I'm the luckiest person on this planet to have your love.

"For those reasons, and through every life change—good or bad—I ask that you accept my commitment to be your best friend, your valentine and the place you call home."

Ben lifted her hands to his lips and kissed them. "I will," he whispered.

Melinda thought her heart would burst with happiness. She went on. "I vow to share your joys and heartaches and give you room to grow.

"I promise to be the mother of your children. And best of all, your wife for as long as I live."

There was a hush when she was through speaking.

Bertie burst into sobs. Joseph rose from his front seat and put his arm around her.

"I just knew they were meant for each other," she sobbed into his shoulder. "It was destiny all along."

Reverend Good beamed at Ben and Melinda. After a moment, he turned to the wedding guests. "Friends, there is little left to be said after such heartfelt wedding vows. So I'll close by asking God's blessing on these two wonderful young people and pronounce them husband and wife."

He did.

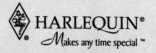

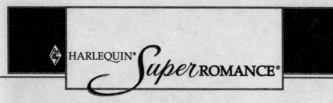

HARLEQUIN *Super* **ROMANCE**

*Here's what small-town dreams
are made of!*

BORN IN A
SMALL TOWN

is a special 3-in-1 collection featuring

New York Times bestselling author
Debbie Macomber's brand-new *Midnight Sons*
title, *Midnight Sons and Daughters*

Judith Bowen's latest *Men of Glory* title—
The Glory Girl

Janice Kay Johnson returns to
Elk Springs, Oregon with *Patton's Daughters*
in *Promise Me Picket Fences*

Join the search for romance in three small towns
in September 2000.

Available at your favorite retail outlet.

HARLEQUIN®
Makes any time special ™

Visit us at www.eHarlequin.com   HSRBORNR

**Don't miss
an exciting opportunity
to save on the purchase of
Harlequin and Silhouette books!**

Buy any two Harlequin or
Silhouette books and save
$10.00 off future Harlequin
and Silhouette purchases

OR

buy any three
Harlequin or Silhouette books
and save **$20.00 off** future
Harlequin and Silhouette purchases.

*Watch for details
coming in October 2000!*

PHQ400

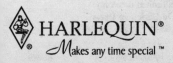

HARLEQUIN
Duets™